## Books in the American Dog series:

*Brave*

*Chestnut*

*Poppy*

# AMERICAN DOG
## ★ STAR ★

BY JENNIFER LI SHOTZ

HOUGHTON MIFFLIN HARCOURT
BOSTON   NEW YORK

hmhbooks.com

Produced by Alloy Entertainment

alloyentertainment

30 Hudson Yard
22nd Floor
New York, NY 10001

The text was set in Adobe Caslon Pro.

Library of Congress Cataloging-in-Publication Data is available.

ISBN: 978-0-358-10871-9 paper over board
ISBN: 978-0-358-10875-7 paperback

Manufactured in the United States of America
DOC 10 9 8 7 6 5 4 3 2 1
4500805196

*For Murph, who taught me how to speak dog*

# ★ CHAPTER 1 ★

**Julian hunched over his desk,** shielding his notebook with his arm. He hoped it looked like he was taking notes as Ms. Hollin introduced the next book the class would be reading. But there were no words on his notebook page, just sketches of trees and lakes and old roads. Julian was trying to recreate one of his favorite maps from memory—an old county map drawn by people who had come to Michigan a hundred years ago searching for Great Lakes treasure.

Julian concentrated on getting the lines just right. He imagined treasure hunters and pirates tromping through town in search of gold. He didn't bother paying attention to the title of the book that everyone in

1

class would be reading over the next month. Everyone except him.

Ms. Hollin called Isabelle and Hunter up to her desk to help pass out the books. The battered paperbacks had probably been read by hundreds of other students. Maybe Julian would get a copy with missing pages, and then he couldn't be blamed for not doing the reading.

He knew he should try to keep up with the assignments, but what was the point? He'd spent his whole life trying to keep up, only to keep falling further and further behind. It wasn't fair. Reading was so easy for other kids, but to him, every page looked like a puzzle with pieces missing. Or worse—like someone had taken five different puzzles and jumbled all the pieces together into one big pile.

Hunter slapped a book on top of Julian's notebook and shot him a smirk before moving on to the next desk. As soon as Hunter wasn't looking, Julian picked up the book to make sure it hadn't smeared his hand-drawn map. That's when he heard Isabelle whisper,

"This is almost twice as long as the last book. There's no way Julian can read it."

"Maybe his mom will read it to him," Hunter whispered back.

"Don't be mean," Isabelle said. But it sounded like she was trying not to laugh.

Julian shoved the book into his backpack without looking at it. He was so tired of the looks and whispers. He was tired of kids like Hunter treating him like he was stupid. He was especially tired of feeling like no matter what he did, reading never seemed to get any easier. He only felt dumber each year.

At least Julian had a name for it now: dyslexia. Over the summer, his parents had taken him to a doctor, who told them that Julian struggled to read because his brain was different from other kids' brains—and that it wasn't his fault.

Not that Hunter cared about any of that.

After the diagnosis, Julian had spent a few days at reading camp—or "stupid kids' camp," as he thought of it—but it all went by so fast that it didn't really help him. Meanwhile all his classmates were outside at soccer camp or going fishing and canoeing in Michigan's clear, cool lakes.

Now that he was back in school, Julian's teachers were giving him more time to do his work, but he still couldn't get the assignments done. And his parents were supposed to take him to see a specialist who could help him, but they'd already spent a ton of money on the camp, and Julian knew the appointment would be expensive too. He was dreading the visits anyway. He pictured himself sitting on a hard-backed chair in a dusty office, staring at the pages of a book while a mean old lady leaned over him and shook her head at his stupidity.

But would an expert even help? Could anyone? Part of him wished his mom *would* read the book with him—or, even better, for him.

At least English was Julian's last class of the day. He had to survive only ten more minutes; then he could forget about books and get back to his maps.

"For tonight, class—" Ms. Hollin called out above the rustling of notebooks and backpacks and zippers, "just read the first two chapters." She started straightening the stack of papers on her desk and cleared her throat.

Julian felt her eyes on him.

He sank lower in his chair. He knew what was coming.

"Julian, please see me after the bell," Ms. Hollin said, tapping the stack of papers. Julian had a sinking feeling that there was supposed to be one with his name on it in the pile.

A few kids snickered. There were more whispers from the back of the classroom, where Hunter sat with his friends. They loved it when Julian got in trouble for not doing his homework, or for not wanting to read out loud in class—which was all the time.

He kept his eyes on the floor, imagining it curving into a slide that would carry him away from school and out to Silver Lake, where he could swim in the cool water and search for bullfrogs in the marshy grasses along the shore. He pictured himself scooping up a fat bullfrog, only to reveal a gold coin from a lost treasure in the mud beneath it.

But the floor stayed flat and boring, except for a small beetle crawling under the desk in front of him. Julian watched the beetle. He knew he should've done the homework. But it felt endless and dumb, like digging a hole in the rain. Eventually, it was easier to just give up and set down the shovel.

The bell rang, and the beetle barely escaped being squished by the stampede of kids leaving the classroom. The bug scurried toward the wall, where it slipped into a crack in the corner and disappeared. Julian wished he could shrink down and follow it.

"Julian."

He looked up. The classroom was empty, and Ms. Hollin had that expression his parents sometimes got, like *couldn't he just try a little harder?* Like it was somehow harder on them than it was on him. It was usually followed by a sigh of disappointment that his dyslexia hadn't magically disappeared.

Julian pulled himself out of his seat, slung his backpack over his shoulder, and went to the front of the room.

"Do you have your signed reading log?" his teacher asked.

Julian's heart dropped. Every week he was supposed to track how much time he spent reading at home and have it signed by his parents so he could turn it in for credit. He pictured the school library book sitting on his bedroom floor, a rumpled T-shirt thrown over it so he didn't have to keep looking at the cover. He'd started reading it. But even after a whole summer at reading camp, it took him forever to get through the first page.

His parents tried to help him after dinner every night, but by then they were both exhausted from long days at work and distracted by everything they needed to do the next day. Every night, as they yawned their way through the lesson with him, he had to ignore the sounds of his brother's video games in the next room. Henry blew through his homework in no time at all and had the whole evening to do whatever he wanted. Julian usually wound up pretending that he understood and telling them he would finish reading on his own, just to let them off the hook. Once they went to bed, he was left alone, staring at the page until he gave up.

Julian had known from the first day back at school that this year was going to be another failure. Just like last year.

"Are you sure I didn't turn it in?" Julian couldn't bring himself to admit that he hadn't even gotten through the first chapter. Some of the other kids were already checking out their second book. He couldn't admit out loud that he was a quitter.

Ms. Hollin tapped the stack of papers. "I don't have it."

"I . . . I'm sure it's here somewhere." Julian began rummaging through his backpack. As he dug through the jumble of books and papers inside the dark mouth of his black canvas bag, his chest filled with frustration, tightening like a balloon ready to pop.

Julian began to stack notebooks and homework sheets on Ms. Hollin's desk. Even though he knew the reading log was blank, he wanted to find it to prove that he was at least responsible. He may not have done the assignment, but he didn't lose things. Maybe he wouldn't get in as much trouble if he showed her that he still had the log.

Julian took out his phone and an old map of the Upper Peninsula that he'd found at a garage sale the previous weekend. He added them to the pile of his books and papers teetering on the edge of Ms. Hollin's desk. Finally, at the very bottom of his bag, he found the reading log. He pulled out the crumpled sheet of paper, hoping against hope that maybe he'd gotten it signed after all. Maybe he'd convinced his dad to give him credit for effort after one of their long evenings at the kitchen table. But the only marking on the sheet was a smudge of dirt.

"I'll do it tonight," he said. "I promise."

Ms. Hollin opened her desk drawer. "This is the third week in a row, Julian."

Julian bit his lip as his teacher pulled out a bright yellow detention slip. He hated that color. It was the yellow of sour lemons and the dandelions his mom made him help her pull from the flower beds every spring. It was the color of his parents' disappointment that, once again, he hadn't been able to keep up.

Ms. Hollin wrote his name in neat block letters at the top of the paper and checked off "Saturday Detention." "I'm sorry, Julian. I know reading isn't as easy for you as it is for the other students, but you still have to complete your assignments. Make sure your parents get this."

Julian slowly put everything back into his bag, carefully setting the bright yellow sheet on top. It was just the beginning of the school year, and it would be his third detention already. He walked home with his head down, feeling ashamed and embarrassed.

He only looked up when he reached the old Winderhouser place. He took the route home along Stagecoach Road almost every day just so he'd pass this way. The leaning two-story house used to be light blue with black shutters, but the paint had gone gray with age, and most of the shutters were missing. The porch sagged under the weight of furniture, appliances, and boxes piled high. Chairs with missing legs, toys faded by the sun, and rusting lawn mowers lay scattered among the tall grass of the yard like hiding animals.

People said a lot of things about the house and about old Mrs. Winderhouser, who used to live there. Some kids claimed that it was haunted or that she had been a witch. Julian didn't believe any of it. His brother, Henry, said mean things about the place — calling it a "firetrap" and "rat heaven." But that's because Henry couldn't see how amazing a little messiness could be.

Julian set his backpack on the ground next to the big maple tree at the edge of the overgrown yard. As he pushed aside books and papers and took his notebook out of his bag, he thought about how boring Henry's neat room was anyway. But the Winderhouser place was full of treasure.

He flipped to the back of his notebook, past the blank pages where his class notes should be, until he reached the sketch he'd started last week. It was a drawing of the crumbling house, as only Julian could see it. He continued penciling in every detail he could make out from his spot by the maple tree, drawing the treasures in the yard and piled on the porch, shading in the dirt and shadows that made all the objects come alive on the page.

As he sketched, he made up stories about where each item had come from and the adventures it had seen before winding up here. He drew the dusty red-and-purple rug that was slumped over the porch railing, imagining it spread out on the floor of a thieves' den. He pictured the broken brass chandelier beside the steps hanging over a long wooden table where knights and kings stuffed themselves on huge feasts.

Julian was almost done mapping out the entire front porch. He'd need to find a new spot where he could see more of the house. He'd gotten in the habit of crouching down by the maple tree because the wide trunk and leafy branches hid him from view, just in case Mrs. Winderhouser ever looked out her window. But he'd heard that she had recently passed away.

The house had always been still and strange, but with no one living there, it seemed as if the whole property had fallen into a deep slumber. Julian glanced up and down the block. He didn't see anyone. He shouldered his backpack, tucked his notebook under his arm, and crept across the yard. He was curious about every object he stepped around, but he'd have to look closer another time. Today, he wanted a glimpse inside. He rounded the side of the house and peered through the window.

Julian gasped. It wasn't just the porch. The room was piled high with boxes, bags, furniture, and trinkets as far as he could see. He began sketching as fast as he could, trying to capture everything. There was just so much. Mrs. Winderhouser was a collector of treasure.

Julian tilted the notebook to get better light on it. He looked up and realized that the shadows falling across the page were from the setting sun. He'd completely lost track of time. He shoved the notebook back into his bag, glanced through the window once more, and took off running. Good thing he was only a few blocks from home or he would have been late for dinner.

He slid into his seat at the round kitchen table across from Henry. His brother scowled at him for being the last one to the table, the same way he did every night, as if he were starving and it was Julian's fault. Julian and his brother had the same narrow face, hazel eyes, and spiky haircuts. It was like looking in a mirror at an older, meaner version of himself.

Julian's parents passed around serving bowls of salad and spaghetti with meatballs. Julian took a piece of garlic bread and sprinkled cheese on his pasta. He'd just finished twirling the perfect forkful of spaghetti when his dad said, "How was school today, Jules?"

The fork slipped from Julian's hand. The spaghetti plopped onto his plate, splattering the tablecloth with red sauce. His mom looked from the spots to Julian's dad to Julian. "Uh-oh," she said. "What happened?"

His face growing warm, Julian pushed his chair back and went to get the detention slip from his backpack. He could feel his cheeks turning red as he handed the yellow sheet of paper to his mom.

"Again?" His mom scanned the words quickly. Julian sank into his chair, wondering if reading had always been easy for her, too. She set the slip next to her plate. "Jules," she said pleadingly. "We've been over this—you just need to keep trying."

"I did try," Julian insisted.

Henry rolled his eyes. Julian glared across the table at his brother.

"We know it's tough for you," his dad said. "But you've got to keep up with your schoolwork."

Julian's shoulders slumped. "I know. I'll try harder."

"Honey, I think we should make an appointment with that specialist—"

Julian cut his mom off. "No—that's okay." He didn't want them to waste any more money. A specialist couldn't help unless he gave Julian an entirely new brain. "I'll try harder—I mean it."

A pained expression flashed across his mom's face. "We know you're trying already, Jules." She sighed and eyed his plate. "Eat, please."

Julian picked up his fork and pushed the spaghetti around, but he had lost his appetite. Silence hung around them for a minute, until Julian finally dropped his fork again with a loud clink.

"Julian!" His dad shook his head. "That's not okay."

With a grim laugh, Julian realized that he couldn't even eat his dinner right. No matter what he was doing, he messed it up. He looked down at the cold lump of meat and noodles and wished he could make it all disappear. If only he had a dog, he could sneak the meatballs under the table and pretend like he'd eaten them. Maybe then he wouldn't get scolded for wasting his dinner on top of getting detention.

Julian had let everyone down. Again. He wished his brain was as good as everyone else's. He swore to himself that he was going to do better . . . somehow.

# ★ CHAPTER 2 ★

**Julian slumped down the hall,** his sneakers scuffing the floor. He had spent his last two detentions helping Ms. Hollin rearrange her classroom bookshelves and cleaning out the storage closet. It was better than having to write an essay on the importance of homework. His teacher last year had made him do that once. By the end of detention, he'd only managed to scratch out a handful of sentences in his crooked handwriting. He had been sent home with a note for his parents and had been grounded for a week for messing up detention—punishment on top of punishment. He hadn't failed on purpose. His teachers and parents just didn't seem to understand that it didn't matter if he *wanted* to do his homework. He couldn't do it.

At least Ms. Hollin left him alone to daydream while he organized books and cleaned shelves. He'd spent the whole time thinking about all the maps in his collection. He wondered if one of them might lead to a treasure that had been left behind by loggers, bank robbers, or pirates. He hoped to visit every single place on those maps, to see what they were like and how they'd changed since they were first plotted on a piece of paper. He wanted to explore the world and record the places he discovered on his own maps. Maybe someone else would look at them and collect them someday, dozens—or even hundreds—of years from now.

Julian's heart sank a little as he looked out the window. The fall weather was perfect, still warm enough to wear a T-shirt, but the air had that sweet apple crispness that meant the leaves would start changing colors soon. Henry was going to the cider mill with his friends for warm cinnamon doughnuts and spiced apple cider. They'd probably chase one another through the corn maze, teasing each other every time they hit a dead end. Ever since they were little, Julian always figured out the maze before anyone else. With one glance, it made sense to him. He'd wait for his family at the end with his arms crossed and a grin on his face. But instead of spending Saturday waiting for his brother and getting to tease Henry for being the slow one for once, Julian was stuck in school.

Julian reached the classroom door and stopped in his tracks. Ms. Hollin wasn't there. Instead, behind her desk sat Mr. Walter. The new principal.

Mr. Walter looked up and gave Julian a smile as warm as the sun shining through the window on his bald head. Instead of his usual dress shirt and tie, Mr. Walter was wearing a maroon polo shirt and khaki pants. He looked like he belonged at a family brunch or on the golf course instead of at school.

"Hi, Julian," Mr. Walter said. "Come on in."

Julian hesitated. "Is Ms. Hollin sick?"

Or was she home planting her garden or sipping lemonade on her porch or whatever teachers did on weekends?

Mr. Walter's presence made Julian nervous. The principal had always been nice to him, but kids were sent to his office only if they were in big trouble. Julian swallowed, feeling the knot in his throat.

Mr. Walter shook his head. "This is your third strike, Julian. That means you get to spend your Saturday with me." His broad forehead wrinkled in a familiar look of exasperation. "Didn't Ms. Hollin write that on your detention slip?"

Julian didn't answer. He didn't want to admit that he hadn't even tried to read the details of his detention. He'd just handed the slip to his parents and accepted his fate.

Mr. Walter adjusted his glasses and nodded toward the middle desk in the front row. Julian dropped into the seat, and the principal handed him a battered classroom copy of *The Giver*. Julian recognized the paperback from when he'd helped rearrange the bookshelves. Mr. Walter picked up a second copy of the book and tapped it against his palm. "We're going to make up your reading assignment today. Every time you finish a chapter, we'll check in and discuss what you read."

Julian's cheeks burned. He didn't want to tell Mr. Walter that it would take him all weekend to read one chapter. He couldn't think of anything worse than having to sit and read in front of the principal. Who could concentrate on a book with someone watching them?

But Julian didn't want to get himself in more trouble by arguing, so he opened the book to chapter one.

His gaze kept slipping from the page to the window. A pair of squirrels chased each other along the branches of a big maple tree. The one with a nut in its mouth disappeared into a hole in the tree trunk, leaving the other one behind. Julian imagined the squirrel standing guard while its friend climbed deep into the tree to bury its treasure. He'd watched a video online about squirrels using landmarks so they wouldn't forget where they stored their food. But what about the ones who had trouble remembering? Maybe there were tiny squirrel-size maps for the forgetful ones.

Mr. Walter cleared his throat loudly.

Julian's head shot back around. "Sorry," he said sheepishly. He sank further in his seat and tried to refocus on the book. He could feel Mr. Walter's eyes on him as he ran his finger along under the words, trying to remember the tips from reading camp. Julian bit his lip and searched the page for a familiar combination of letters. He just needed somewhere to start. He sneaked a glance at Mr. Walter. The principal was watching him with a furrowed brow.

Julian felt sweat break out on *his* brow. He squirmed and stared at the page again, struggling through the first couple of pages. Mr. Walter had started typing on the computer on Ms. Hollin's desk. The *click-clack* of the keys was distracting. So were the *hmmm* noises Mr. Walter made in the back of his throat.

Finally, after what felt like forever, the principal pushed back the desk chair and stood up. "Okay. I can see this isn't going to work."

Julian shot up straight in his chair. He couldn't fail detention. "No—I'm reading. Really, I am. Please, I —" He didn't know how to finish the sentence.

Mr. Walter studied him for a long moment, as if he were trying to make sense of something. Julian couldn't read his expression. Was he angry at Julian, like everyone else always was? Or was he just frustrated? Was he thinking of a way to tell Julian's mom that her son had failed detention too?

"Will you be okay on your own for a minute?" Mr. Walter asked. "I need to make a quick phone call."

Julian nodded, dropping his eyes to the puzzle pieces spilled across the pages of his book. But once Mr. Walter was gone, he couldn't help watching the door. The principal's low voice rumbled in the hallway. It got louder, then softer as Mr. Walter paced in front of the classroom door. Julian couldn't make out what he was saying, but he had a sinking feeling that it had to do with him. Was he about to get into even bigger trouble? But for what? He'd shown up for detention like he was supposed to. Julian's brain twisted around on itself with worry and uncertainty.

When the doorknob turned, Julian ducked his head and flipped ahead a few pages. He tried to look absorbed in the chapter. Mr. Walter towered over

Julian's desk. He held out a hand for the book. "I'm sorry, Julian."

Julian tried to hold on to the book, as if that would prove he was being responsible. He didn't want Mr. Walter to give up on him. "I'm trying. I really am."

"I know you are." Mr. Walter gently pulled the book from Julian's hands. "You can check this out if you want to read it at home, but I've got a different idea."

"Are there more closets to clean?" Julian glanced longingly at the sunlight sparkling off the empty desk-tops. He'd rather move around than just sit here, but he didn't want to spend the day in some dark, window-less room.

Mr. Walter chuckled, his shoulders bobbing up and down. "No closets. But maybe some kennels."

"Kennels?" Julian's attention snapped from the sunlight to his principal.

"You like dogs, don't you?" Mr. Walter asked.

"Yes. I don't have one or anything, but I've always . . . wanted one." Confusion filled Julian's voice. What did dogs have to do with his reading assignment?

Mr. Walter pulled out the chair at the desk beside

Julian and sat down. He leaned forward, his elbows on his knees. "I just talked to your mom."

Julian's face felt tight. His mom spent every Saturday helping Grandpa around the house. They went grocery shopping and prepared meals so Grandpa would have enough to eat for the week. She wouldn't be happy if she had to leave because he'd messed up detention again.

"She told me about your challenges," Mr. Walter said gently.

Julian's nervousness was quickly replaced by shame. Now the new principal knew he was stupid. He'd probably want to hold him back a grade or put him in special classes. Julian didn't know what to say. He hated talking about his reading problems.

"There's nothing to be ashamed of, Julian. Lots of kids have dyslexia. Ten percent in fact." Mr. Walter hefted Julian's book in his hand.

Julian tried to change the subject. "What about dogs and kennels?"

Mr. Walter's serious expression broke into a wide smile. "Who doesn't love dogs, right? There's an animal shelter on the other side of town. Your mom said it was okay if we took a little field trip. So what do you say we go check it out?"

"She did?" Julian looked up at Mr. Walter, his head tilted in surprise. A field trip was the last thing he'd expected.

"We agreed that it might be a good change of pace for you." Mr. Walter stood and set the book down on Ms. Hollin's desk. He took his keys out of his pocket. "My son Bryan volunteers there. He really loves it."

Julian didn't know Bryan Walter very well, as the Walter family had moved to town only a few months earlier. But they had a couple of classes together. Julian wasn't the most popular kid in school, but Bryan was seriously uncool. He was always the first to raise his hand in class, pouncing on questions like a cat on a mouse. In his weirdly booming voice, he gave the longest answers, full of memorized dates and names. And whenever he turned in an assignment, he thanked the teacher for giving him homework. At lunch, Bryan sat by himself, with huge headphones over his ears and his nose in a book. Julian couldn't imagine that they had anything in common.

He didn't think he could stand to spend an entire Saturday with Bryan Walter. But anything was better than being stuck in an empty school, alone with the principal. And he really did love dogs. He'd been asking his parents for years if they could get one.

Before Mr. Walter could change his mind, Julian leaped out of his seat and headed toward the door. "Let's go!"

# ★ CHAPTER 3 ★

**The animal shelter lobby** was painted a cheery creamsicle orange, with framed photos of dogs and cats and colorful posters about friendship and flea prevention lining the walls. It reminded Julian of a kindergarten classroom. Well, except for the flea prevention. The woman sitting behind the counter had straight black hair pulled into a thick ponytail. She greeted them with a wide smile.

"This is Ms. Khan," Mr. Walter said. "She keeps this place running."

"More like it keeps me running." Ms. Khan's laugh was as bright as the walls. "It's nice to meet you, Julian. Have you been to the shelter before?"

Julian shook his head. Every time he'd asked for a dog, his parents had said they were too busy. He'd asked once if they could just visit the shelter dogs, but they'd said they didn't want to get his hopes up.

Ms. Khan clapped her hands. "Welcome! I'll take you back to the kennels, and then Bryan can help show you the ropes."

"Thanks." Julian couldn't help returning her smile. He was excited to see the dogs. For once, he felt like he was being rewarded instead of punished. But as they pushed through double doors into a long hallway, he started to feel nervous. What if he wasn't good with the animals? What would he and Bryan talk about all day? What if Bryan thought he was stupid for being in detention?

Julian slowed his steps. Almost as if Ms. Khan sensed his worry, she glanced over her shoulder to make sure he was following her. He shot her an anxious smile and scrambled to catch up. Out of the corner of his eye, he saw a row of flyers fixed to the wall, each one showing off a different dog or cat up for adoption at the shelter.

About halfway down the hallway Ms. Khan paused at a giant window set in the wall. Julian stopped next to her and peered into a small room. Just on the other side of the glass he saw a tall, narrow structure—like a large coat rack with shelves—covered in beige carpet. Behind it was an armchair and a low bookshelf. Cats sprawled on every bare surface.

"We call this room our cat condo," Ms. Khan said. "It helps potential adopters see what these guys might be like in a home. Someday, I hope all our cats can be in condos, but for now, it gives a few at a time a break from their cages."

Julian counted at least six cats scattered and lounging around the room. A lanky black cat hopped up onto the highest shelf of the cat tree, just inches from Julian's face, and lazily swatted at the glass. Julian laughed and tapped the window with his finger. The cat pawed at him from the other side.

"That's Cleopatra," Ms. Khan said. "I think she likes you."

Cleopatra batted at Julian's fingers dancing along the glass. When he looked up, Ms. Khan was on the move again. With one last tap for his new cat friend, he hurried to catch up.

Ms. Khan led him through a metal door into a long room lined floor to ceiling with cages on three walls.

"More cats." Ms. Khan said, stating the obvious with a grin.

Julian had never seen anything like it. Each cage held a skinny, rotund, sleepy, playful, happy, or grumpy-looking cat. A man stood in front of an open cage door, scooping a litter box. He seemed to barely notice the small brindle kitten perched on his shoulder. One or two of the cats twitched their heads in Julian's direction, and a fat orange tabby with white paws ducked his head in greeting.

They stepped out and headed farther down the hall. Ms. Khan turned a corner into another hallway. She paused in front of three windowed doors that opened into three small spaces.

"These are our meet-and-greet rooms, where people can get to know an animal before they adopt one," she said.

Julian peered inside. Each room was nearly filled

with an overstuffed armchair and a basket of dog toys, waiting for games of tug of war.

They continued past a series of doors without windows. The one that smelled sharply of bleach was probably a storage closet, Julian thought. The next one was partially open, and it rumbled as if it were holding back a train. He could see laundry tumbling around in machines that looked big enough to eat the washer and dryer his parents had at home.

Julian felt like he was in a maze, his only signposts the smell of floor cleaner, fur, and kibble. His fingers tingled with the urge to map it out, but he'd left his backpack and notebooks in Mr. Walter's car.

Ms. Khan turned another corner, bringing them closer to the muffled sound of barking. When they finally stopped in front of the dog room, she turned to face Julian, her expression still warm but serious. "You'll find Bryan right through there. He's been volunteering with us for a while, so follow his lead. But everyone who walks through those doors has to take responsibility. You don't know these dogs, and they don't know you. So don't stick your fingers in the cages. And never go into a cage or take a dog out without permission. Got it?"

Julian nodded. "I understand."

"Good. I have to finish some paperwork, then I'll be back to see how you're doing." Ms. Khan started back down the hallway.

"Thank you—" Julian called after her. She waved and disappeared back around the corner, leaving him to find Bryan in the kennel.

Julian was pleased that Ms. Khan trusted him to be around the animals. He was determined to prove that he was responsible enough to deserve that trust. He wiped his palms on his jeans and opened the door. At the sound of the hinges, two dozen dogs ceased their barking and raised their heads in unison to look at him from their kennels. Each kennel was fairly large, like a dog-size hotel room, outfitted with a water dish and a bed that sort of looked like a trampoline. They lined the walls of the long, narrow room. Julian held his breath as he took in the array of animals in all sizes and colors, all different fur textures and ear shapes. Before he could exhale, the dogs took up their loud barking again, as if they were greeting him.

Julian's ears vibrated with the sound, but he stepped forward to say hi to the dogs. The medium-size mutt in the first kennel stood on her hind legs, with her front paws perched on the door. She was all black, except for one white paw, as if she'd stepped in paint. In the next kennel, a beagle bayed at Julian, sounding like a siren. A yellow Lab was too busy tearing up his blanket to pay much attention. But the tan pit bull in the next kennel gazed up so hopefully that Julian had to stop and say hello to her. At the sound of his voice, her tail whipped back and forth so quickly that her whole body wriggled. She licked at the kennel door. The German shepherd in the next kennel whined for Julian to notice him.

Julian thought he could spend all day talking to the dogs and getting to know them. Each kennel had a pale green sign hooked to the door, with writing on it. Julian guessed that each one spelled out the dog's name, breed, age, and other information. Every few cages, he paused to try to read the signs. From what he could tell, one dog was named Bumble. Another liked to play with soccer balls.

Finally, after Julian stepped through a door at the back of the room to find yet another huge space packed with kennels, he found Bryan. He was sitting cross-legged on the floor in front of a cage about two-thirds of the way down a row. His head was bowed, and with his curly hair shielding his face, Julian couldn't tell what he was doing.

Julian got closer and saw a book lying in Bryan's lap.

Without looking at Julian, Bryan held up a finger, telling him to wait. "I just want to finish this chapter for Pip."

He turned a page and continued reading aloud. Julian rolled his eyes, even though he felt like his brother, Henry, when he did it. Had Mr. Walter played some kind of trick on him? Was this how he was supposed to make up his reading assignment? The dogs broke out into a new chorus of barks that echoed up and down the row of kennels. Julian couldn't hear Bryan, and he figured Pip couldn't either. But what did it matter? Julian didn't think that Pip or any of the other dogs cared what happened at the end of the chapter.

But as Julian peered into the kennel in front of Bryan, he saw that the small, scruffy caramel-colored dog inside was watching Bryan attentively. He wasn't at the front of his kennel like most of the other dogs, trying to see what was going on outside. Instead, he lay calmly on his blanket with his head tipped to one side, as if he were really listening to the story.

While Bryan kept reading, Julian waited and watched, wondering how long Bryan expected him to stand there. He considered taking himself on a tour of the rest of the shelter, but he worried that he'd get in trouble and wind up back in detention at school. He'd been told to follow Bryan's lead, so he knew he'd better stay close.

Julian walked back to the first kennel by the door and, trying to kill time, made himself read every word on the pale green sign. The black dog with the white-dipped paw waited patiently while he learned that her name was Rocket and that she'd been a stray. When he finished reading, he rewarded himself by squatting down to say hello to Rocket through the kennel door.

Then he read the next sign. And the next, until he had made his way down the entire row. He learned a dozen dogs' names and ages and how long they'd been at the shelter. He read the cards slowly, but none of the dogs made him feel rushed or like they were judging him. The Lab stopped shredding his blanket and leaned against the kennel door while Julian read about how he'd had too much energy for his previous family. Even the beagle on the bottom row quieted down, sniffing at Julian's jeans through the crate until Julian finished reading and dropped to his knees to give her attention.

The personality sections of the dogs' signs were the best part: "Energetic goofball." "Shy at first, but a real snuggler once she gets to know you!" "Playful pup who needs an active—and we mean *active!*—home." "Laid-back gentle giant." Julian couldn't help but wonder what adjectives would be on his own sign.

When he reached Bryan again, he noticed that Pip's sign was white instead of green. He waited until

Bryan paused between sentences. "Why is his a different color?" Julian asked.

Bryan ignored him until he finished reading the page. Julian crossed his arms and tried to wait patiently.

"That's it for now, Pip," Bryan said, standing slowly, brushing loose dog fur off his jeans, and tucking the book under his arm. Then he finally turned to Julian. "White means he needs extra attention. He's really scared and doesn't want to go on walks yet. So I read to him to get him used to having people around. Reading helps the other dogs calm down, too."

Julian opened his mouth to say that sounded ridiculous, but he noticed for the first time that the dogs in the kennels next to Pip were lying quietly by their kennel doors. It seemed that Bryan was right.

"I'll show you around," Bryan said. "Then we can finish cleaning."

Bryan had something to say about every single dog as he led Julian past their cages. He knew whether they preferred treats or tennis balls, whether they pulled on the leash or rolled over for belly rubs. As usual, he acted like he knew everything about everything. Julian trailed behind him, trying to picture what each dog would be like in his house. He thought the tall hound with floppy ears would sleep at the foot of his bed and probably snore. But the reddish-brown dog that looked like a fox would probably tear all the stuffing out of his pillow. He tried to guess if the shepherd mix, with one ear standing straight up and the other one flopped over, was already potty-trained or if she'd pee in Henry's bedroom.

They had reached the end of the last row when Bryan pointed toward an empty kennel on the bottom.

"This is Star," Bryan said without stopping.

The kennel had only looked empty. When Julian stopped in front of it and bent over to peer inside, he spotted a medium-size dog curled up into a tight ball in the back corner of her cage. She wore a faded pink collar, and her white fur blended in with the white blanket she slept on. Unlike the other dogs, her ears didn't perk up or twitch as the boys talked in front of her crate. She had a white kennel sign, like Pip, but there was almost nothing written on it.

Julian got down on the floor to take a closer look, accidentally bumping his knee on the kennel door, making it rattle. The dog startled and looked out at him with wary blue eyes, as if noticing him for the first time. She hunched deeper into the corner, trembling so much it sent a small ripple through her soft-looking fur.

"Wait—" Julian called after Bryan. "What about this one? What does she like?"

Bryan turned back and sighed. "No one knows. She won't let anyone near her. We can't even take off her collar . . . she won't let us."

"Does reading to her help?" Julian was half joking —but also kind of curious.

Bryan shook his head. "She's deaf."

"Oh," Julian said, surprised. He felt silly, but it had never occurred to him before that dogs could be deaf. He tried to imagine what life was like there for her in the noisy kennel. He didn't know what would be scarier—the racket or the silence.

"She's the most difficult case in the shelter right now," Bryan said.

"Why?" Julian asked. "Because she can't hear?"

"It's not just that," Bryan said. "She doesn't trust anyone. Until she came here, she'd never even been outside. No one ever gave her any training. She'd never been on a leash or gone to the vet. She never even saw people other than her owner."

Star pulled her legs in beneath her, curling up again without taking her eyes off the boys. Julian's chest tightened. Star had to be the loneliest, most misunderstood dog in the world. "How did she end up here?"

"Her owner died," Bryan said. "I guess Mrs. Winderhouser lived in this big house on Stagecoach Road, and no one even knew she had a dog."

Julian's breath caught in his throat. He leaned forward to get a closer look at Mrs. Winderhouser's dog. He searched his memory for signs of Star at the house, trying to remember if there were any dog toys or bowls in the map he'd drawn of the old place.

Bryan gave Star a long, sad look. "Everyone says she's untrainable." He turned to walk away.

Julian nodded as if he agreed, but as he and the scruffy dog held each other's gaze for a moment, a strange feeling began wriggling in his gut—a hunch that there was more to this dog than anyone knew. He thought of all the times he had felt misjudged by the world. Maybe, Julian thought, Star felt the same way.

As if in response, the dog licked her muzzle and sighed. She seemed to relax a little as she followed Bryan with her eyes, but her expression remained alert. Her nose twitched like a rabbit's. Julian had the sense that she didn't miss anything that happened around her, even if she couldn't hear.

His mind whirred with questions. Where had Mrs. Winderhouser gotten Star? Had she been a puppy? What was it like for Star to live in that house that was full of rooms and things to explore? He imagined her clambering over boxes and squeezing under furniture, her white fur bright in the shadowy house.

As Julian started to stand up to follow Bryan, Star raised her head and watched him. Julian was sure he saw a glimmer in her bright blue eyes. He imagined that she didn't want him to go. Maybe she hoped that each new person who stopped at her kennel would be the one who finally understood her. He squatted down again so he was at her eye level.

"Hi, girl," he whispered. Star shifted and sniffed the air, her bright eyes meeting his. Julian bet that she was waiting for someone to see the real her, the same way he often wanted, for once, not to be overlooked. He suspected that Star was the greatest treasure Mrs. Winderhouser had ever found.

# ★ CHAPTER 4 ★

**Ms. Khan returned** to give Julian the full behind-the-scenes tour of the shelter. She showed him the kennels that held newly arrived dogs, where only staff and volunteers were allowed to go. She showed him the grooming room, the laundry room, the kitchen, the socialization room, the administrative offices, and every closet that held spare cages, food, kitty litter, potty-training pads, and other supplies.

Bryan came along, practically leading the tour himself. He knew every nook and cranny of the building, and now Julian did too, as if he had joined a special club.

"The more you volunteer with us, the more

responsibilities you'll be able to take on," said Ms. Khan as she led them into an industrial kitchen. The metal counters were loaded to the brim with empty food bowls. "For now, you'll start with tasks that require less training, and we'll work your way up to working with the animals."

Julian nodded vigorously to show that he was eager to take on more responsibility.

"Today I'd like to have you help me in here," she said, waving to the stack of dirty bowls. Julian's eyes widened at the towering pile. "If you can help me get this under control, I'll teach you some of the basics of dog handling before you head home."

Julian kept his smile fixed and tried not to show his disappointment. He had hoped that he'd get to work with the animals that day, or at least talk with them, like Bryan got to. He cast a sidelong glance at Bryan, who was already thumbing for the place where he left off in his book. Maybe the principal had told Ms. Khan about Julian's reading challenges and she thought he was too stupid to read to the animals. His cheeks suddenly felt hot.

As if she could read his mind, Ms. Khan's face softened. "Don't worry, Julian. Everyone starts out doing the least glamorous jobs. You'll get to work with the animals in no time."

After Ms. Khan finished the tour, the boys got to work. Bryan left Julian in the kitchen to wash dishes while he went outside to hose down cages. Julian stared at the dozens of stainless-steel food and water bowls piled haphazardly in the sink and on the countertops. He groaned. He'd never seen so many dishes in his life. It wasn't fair that Bryan got to be outside in the sunshine while he had to wash a million bowls. But Julian was the one who was supposed to be in detention, so he turned on the faucet and started scrubbing.

As he worked, it seemed like the bowls were multiplying on the counters around him, as if they'd been cursed by an evil wizard. He tried to pretend that every time he cleared part of the counter, he took some of the wizard's power. He hoped the story would distract him, but his mind kept drifting back to Star, curled up in her kennel. It made him sad to think that no one had been able to get through to her.

There had to be a way.

Julian shut off the faucet and stuck his head into the hallway. Ms. Khan had come to check up on him about twenty bowls ago and she said he was doing a great job, so hopefully she wouldn't mind if he took a little break. He made his way through the maze of hallways toward Star's kennel. He'd mapped out the shelter in his head during the tour. All he had to do was follow it back to where X marked the spot for Star.

She was still huddled in the corner of her kennel. She looked like she was napping, but her eyes snapped open as Julian lowered himself to the ground in front of her cage. A soft, uncertain growl rumbled from her throat.

"It's okay," Julian said. "You don't have to be afraid of me."

Her growl grew louder. He wished he knew how to tell her she was safe. He pressed his palm flat against the cage door. The dog flinched at his movement, but then her gaze flicked from Julian's hand to his eyes. She'd probably had so many people walk by her cage without looking at her that she wasn't sure what to make of this sudden attention. Julian stayed still, trying to communicate that he understood. Her growl rose into soft whimper.

Julian held his breath as Star pushed herself off her blanket and took a tentative step forward. Now that she wasn't curled up in a ball, he could see that she wasn't really all white. Patches of light gray fur melded with darker gray splotches on her back. The pattern almost looked like one of his old maps. Star inched closer to him, her head and long, fluffy tail low.

Julian's whole body was humming with excitement, but he made himself sit perfectly still. Star took another step forward, as if she were moving in slow motion. He'd heard that dogs didn't like to be stared at, so he kept his eyes on her paws as she crept closer. She had little tufts of white fur between her toes and light gray speckles on her back feet.

Star stopped just a few inches from the door of the crate. Julian still wasn't looking right at her, but he could hear her sniffing the air, trying to pick up his scent. It was hard not to look into her bright, intelligent blue eyes. He breathed as slowly as he could, trying not to scare her back to the corner. Her paws inched forward again. When she reached the kennel door, she stretched her neck out and sniffed the palm of Julian's hand.

"That's a good girl," he whispered. For a few seconds, he felt her cold nose and warm breath snuffling against his palm as she examined his hand. When she was done, she sat back and leaned against the side wall of the kennel, just far enough away that he couldn't stick his fingers through the cage and touch her. But she was close enough that he could read the heart-shaped tag on her collar. On it were her name and the numbers 11-25-15.

Julian leaned closer to make sure he'd read the numbers right. November 25th was his birthday! What if that was Star's birthday, too?

Maybe her life hadn't been perfect cooped up inside the big, cluttered house with only Mrs. Winderhouser for company, but Mrs. Winderhouser had loved Star enough to get her a tag to celebrate her birthday.

Star yawned, her pink tongue unfurling from her mouth. She stretched out against the wall of her cage, her front paws inches from the kennel door where Julian sat. Julian felt something stir inside him. He didn't have a lot of experience with dogs. Everything he knew about them was from silly videos online or his grandpa's stories about pups he'd had when he was a boy. He didn't know nearly as much as Ms. Khan, or even Bryan, who had said that Star was untrainable. But deep down, Julian knew he could help this dog.

Julian knew what it was like to be misunderstood. Everyone underestimated him just because his brain didn't work the same way as theirs. His parents loved him, of course, and tried to help, but they didn't know how. Teachers called him difficult. Other kids thought he was weird or stupid. If he was a dog, he'd probably be called untrainable.

Julian could tell from the way Star watched him that she was smart. She just needed someone who believed in her. He wished he could bring her home and give her the life she deserved.

At home after dinner, Julian sat at the kitchen table, his homework spread out in front of him. Henry was in the living room playing online video games and talking to his friends through his headset, his homework finished hours ago. Julian hated how easy school was for his brother. It wasn't fair.

Julian's mom was finishing up the dishes while his dad tried to help him with his history assignment. They were reading an article about the Civil War, but his dad—who'd just come off a double shift at his nursing job at the hospital—kept yawning. Julian could tell he was ready for bed. His dad was rushing through paragraphs to get to the end of the assignment, and the words were a blur for Julian. He just couldn't keep up. It didn't help that his mind kept wandering back to the shelter and the way Star had looked at him.

Julian and his dad finally finished the assignment, and his dad let out a relieved sigh. Julian shoved his books back into his bag, trying to figure out how to talk to his parents about Star. His dad leaned back in his chair and stretched. Any second now, he'd head up to bed. His mom turned off the faucet and hung up the dishtowel. This was Julian's chance.

"Could I get a dog?"

He held his breath, hoping they wouldn't laugh at him. He'd stayed quiet at dinner because he hadn't wanted to say anything in front of Henry. Last year, when Julian wanted to play a game to win a goldfish at the county fair, his brother had said, "Are you kidding? You couldn't even take care of a pet rock!" Julian's parents hadn't said outright that they agreed with Henry, but the only games they let Julian play were the ones with stuffed animals as prizes.

His dad didn't laugh. But he didn't answer right away either. He stifled a yawn behind his hand. Julian's mom leaned against the kitchen counter. "Our plates are so full, Jules. We just can't add anything else."

"What if I took care of her?" Julian asked. "She could be my dog."

He wished he could explain how special Star was, and how much she needed him. But before he could find the words, his mom shook her head. "Dogs are a lot of work. You have to take them outside and train them and remember to feed them . . ."

"I know," Julian said.

"A dog is a living thing that depends on you," his

mom said. "It needs you every day, even when things are tough. It's a much bigger deal than missing a homework assignment."

"I wouldn't give up on a dog," Julian insisted. "This is important."

"Your schoolwork is important, too," she said.

"It's not the same." Not only were Star and homework totally different, but to Julian, the shelter and school didn't even belong on the same planet. He'd felt welcomed and safe at the shelter. At school he was on edge all day.

"You've had a hard enough time as it is," she said. "We don't want to put even more responsibility on you."

Julian knew she was trying to be sympathetic, but somehow that only made it worse. He heard Henry crowing from the other room—"Nice one, dude!"—praising one of his friends in the game. Julian never got to do anything fun. He never got to do things he was actually good at. All he ever did was struggle with his schoolwork, and he never, ever seemed to catch up.

"I hear you did well at the shelter today," his dad said, trying to make him feel better.

"I really liked it," Julian said. "But it was lots of hard work," he added quickly. He didn't want his parents to think he'd had too much fun when he was supposed to be in detention.

He might not be able to adopt Star, but he had a backup plan—at least a way to get to spend time with her.

"I want to keep volunteering at the shelter," he said quietly. He was afraid his parents were going to tell him no again. They were silent for a moment, as if they were having a wordless conversation with each other before responding.

"You need to get your homework done," his dad finally said.

Julian fought a smile. That wasn't a *no*.

"I will," Julian promised. "I can go to the shelter after school and on weekends and still do homework after dinner."

He pictured Star's light blue eyes following him as he left the kennel earlier that day. They had sat quietly for a long time, with just the kennel door between them. All the noise of the shelter and the stress of his life had seemed to fade into the background. When he stood up to go, she got to her feet and watched him walk away. Star needed his help.

His mom shot his dad a meaningful look, her eyebrows raised. "Mr. Walter did say his son has been volunteering at the shelter, and it's been good for him."

Julian had no idea what Bryan had to do with anything, but if the principal thought volunteering was a good idea, his parents had to agree.

His dad shrugged. "If it doesn't get in the way of your schoolwork, I don't see why not."

His mom turned back to Julian. "Okay. We'll give it a test run. But you have to stay on top of your homework. And if you can prove that you're ready for this much responsibility, maybe—*maybe*—we'll think about the dog."

Julian wanted to leap out of his chair, pump his fist in the air, and let out a happy shout. *They hadn't said no!*

But he knew his parents might not think he was responsible if he got so excited. He stayed as cool as could be and hugged his mom, smiling so big that his cheeks hurt. "Thank you, guys!"

She hugged him back. "No promises. But we'll think about it."

Julian would work harder than he ever had in his life. He'd do whatever it took to bring Star home.

# ★ CHAPTER 5 ★

**Julian's heart was racing** as he pedaled his bike down the long road leading to the animal shelter. He could still barely believe that he'd convinced his parents to let him come back on his own. "I'm impressed," his mom had said over their bowls of oatmeal and bananas that morning. "You must really be serious about taking on more responsibility if you want to volunteer."

Julian hadn't corrected her. He *was* serious about being more responsible. But he wasn't interested in just washing dog bowls and hosing down cages. And he definitely wasn't stoked to be spending all his free time with Bryan.

The truth was, he hadn't been able to stop thinking

about Star and that look in her eyes—as if she just wanted someone to understand her. He couldn't stop thinking about the birthday tag on her collar, and how much Mrs. Winderhouser must have loved her. His heart broke to think about how Star must miss the old lady and the house full of treasures they shared.

The low beige building of the shelter appeared on the horizon, and Julian's stomach began to churn with worry. What if Star was different from what he thought she was? He remembered how he thought he loved frozen pizza, but when he tried it after not having it for a long time, it tasted like salty cardboard. Or worse, what if she didn't remember him and she cowered in the corner of her kennel forever?

He hopped off his bike before it rolled to a stop and wheeled it around to the side of the building. The back entrance was propped open by the hose. Julian knew he should probably go through the front door to tell Ms. Khan that he'd come back to volunteer. But if she put him to work right away, it might be hours before he saw Star. He couldn't wait that long. He would just let

Star know he'd come back for her, and then he'd find Ms. Khan. Forcing himself not to run, he practically stumbled through the kennel door and went straight to Star's cage.

His face broke into a huge grin. "Hey there, Star."

She stood near the front of her kennel, watching him, her head cocked. It was almost as if she'd been waiting. She couldn't have heard him coming, though. Maybe she'd felt the vibrations through the floor, or maybe she'd smelled him, especially with the trickle of sweat running down his back from bicycling so fast. Julian wondered just how strong a dog's sense of smell was. He bet that Bryan would know the answer.

Julian's mind was suddenly dancing in a million different directions at once. It was as if he'd been saving up things to say to Star, and every thought was clamoring to get out at the same time. He knelt in front of her cage and began babbling, even though she couldn't hear his voice. He gestured as he told her about himself and his family and how he'd wanted a dog for so long. Her bright eyes followed his hands, occasionally glancing back at his face. He noticed that if he made too big a movement, she flinched, so he was careful to keep his gestures small.

Finally Julian's thoughts slowed to a trickle. He exhaled, his heart rate returning to normal. He shifted so he was sitting in front of her kennel, and he put his hand against the door the way he had the day before. Star inched toward him. She was still cautious, but she didn't hesitate as much as she had yesterday. When she was almost at the kennel door, she stretched out her muzzle. He felt her tongue tickle his palm, as quick and light as a moth fluttering against his skin. Julian was careful to stay still so he wouldn't scare her, but his chest nearly burst with happiness and hope.

He lowered his head so that he was nearly at eye level with her. Star tilted her snout toward his face, her nose working overtime. She was probably smelling the oatmeal he'd had for breakfast. His grandpa told him that dogs could also smell if you were afraid or nervous or excited. Maybe Star's nose was telling her everything about him. When she'd gotten all the information she needed, she moved toward his hand again. Julian waited for another one of her gentle licks.

Then Star startled, scuttling back to the corner of her cage and staring past him with wide eyes. Julian whipped around to find Ms. Khan standing behind him. She tipped her head toward the door. With a glance at Star and a silent promise that he'd be back, Julian followed Ms. Khan past the barking dogs and into the quieter hallway.

She wasn't smiling like she had been the day before. "How did you get in here, Julian? I didn't see you come in the front door."

Julian opened his mouth, then snapped it shut. If Bryan had left the back door open when he was cleaning cages, Julian didn't want to get him into trouble.

Ms. Khan waved a hand. "It doesn't matter. What are you doing here? Did you forget something yesterday?"

"I was hoping I could volunteer again," Julian said.

"You loved detention that much?" Ms. Khan arched an eyebrow. "Better not tell Principal Walter."

"It was a lot better than writing an essay," Julian said.

Ms. Khan laughed. "I can understand that. I'm glad you wanted to come back. But you can't just go wandering around the kennels without checking in with me first, okay?"

"Yes, ma'am." Julian's stomach knotted up. He was afraid he'd be told he couldn't spend any more time with Star. "I didn't have my fingers in her kennel. I swear."

"I know. I saw." Ms. Khan looked at him thoughtfully.

Julian tried not to squirm under her gaze. "So, can I become a volunteer?"

"We have rules for our volunteers." She held up her hand, ticking off each rule on a different finger. "Always check in with me at the beginning and end of your shift. Never open a cage unless you've been approved to work with that animal. Stay alert, and trust your gut. Dress appropriately. No sandals or shorts allowed. And if you see a mess, clean it up. You got all that?"

Julian nodded. "I think so."

He followed Ms. Khan to the kitchen. She pointed to a poster behind the door. "If you ever forget, the ground rules are listed right here. Or you could just ask Bryan."

"Got it." Julian repeated the rules in his head so he would know them by heart. He was glad she'd told him what they were instead of making him read them first.

"Great." Ms. Khan rubbed her hands together. "If you're ready to get started, I have just the thing for you."

Julian had a sneaking suspicion that he'd be stuck washing towers of dirty dog bowls again. He'd peeked into the kitchen on his way to Star's cage, and the piles were just as high as yesterday, as if he'd never been there. But he had to do whatever it took, even if it meant starting with the worst jobs. He stood straighter. "I'll do anything."

Ms. Khan glanced down the hallway toward the kennels. "You went back to visit Star, huh?"

"I'm sorry I didn't check in with you first," Julian

blurted. "I just really like her and wanted to say hi. Then I was going to come find you. I swear."

Ms. Khan waved away his apology. "I haven't seen her get that close to anyone since she got here. Not even me, and I feed her twice a day. You two might have a real connection."

"You really think so?" Julian's pulse raced. If Ms. Khan saw the connection, then it hadn't just been his imagination.

"I do," Ms. Khan said. "And that means you might be able to help her in a way no one else can."

Julian flushed with pride. "She seems like a really cool dog. I mean, she's so scared, but there's something else underneath that."

Ms. Khan smiled and furrowed her brow at the same time. "I think so, too. But I can't seem to get through to her. That's why I have a special assignment for you. I want you to help me work with Star so she gets comfortable enough to be around people."

Julian felt like he might break into a goofy dance. "I can do that!"

This was his chance. He could help Star *and* show

his parents that he was capable of taking on a special assignment. If he did a good job training the dog, maybe his parents would be convinced that he was responsible enough to keep her.

"I'll go get Star from her kennel and meet you in the socialization room. She'll be scared, so don't try to approach her. Just let her get used to being in a room with you, and I'll talk you through the rest." Ms. Khan waited for his nod, then took a leash from a hook on the wall and headed toward the kennel.

Julian wished he could be there to see Star come out of her cage, but he knew he had to follow instructions. He weaved his way through the hallways, following the map in his head to the socialization room. He remembered it from his tour of the shelter.

Bryan was already in there, rearranging the chairs.

The socialization room was almost as big as Julian's bedroom. It had five metal folding chairs along one wall and a dog bed and basket of toys in the corner. Bryan had told him that volunteers and staff used this room to hang out with dogs who were too scared to go outside, or for training and playtime when the weather was freezing in the winter. It was also used as another meet-and-greet room for people to visit with animals they might want to adopt, so they could get to know them outside of the cages. A door at the far end of the room opened into a small office, where Ms. Khan could complete adoption paperwork while families played with the dog or cat they'd fallen in love with.

"Hi," Julian said with an awkward wave.

"Hi."

"What are you doing here?" Julian asked.

"I heard Ms. Khan talking to you and thought I'd help." Bryan picked up a chair and carried it to the opposite side of the room. "We should spread out these chairs so Star doesn't feel like we're crowding her."

Julian moved a chair to the corner by the dog bed. Bryan pointed a few feet away. "Leave room around the dog bed in case Star wants to make that her space. We want her to feel safe." Julian followed Bryan's directions. It made sense. When the chairs were all spread out, Bryan put a handful of crumbled dog treats in Julian's palm. "You'll need these."

Before Julian could respond, the door opened and Star pulled Ms. Khan into the room. The dog's eyes were wide and terrified. She jerked at the end of the leash like a car fishtailing on ice. Julian's stomach tightened. Star was so upset, and there was nothing he could do about it. Ms. Khan talked softly to the dog, but it was clear that Star just wanted to get away.

"She's never been on a leash," Ms. Khan reminded the boys. "We're working on it, but it's hard when she's so scared of everyone. I'm going to go sit down, but you stay on that side of the room until I tell you."

Julian and Bryan nodded, frozen in place near the dog bed. Star kept pulling and flailing at the end of the leash until Ms. Khan sat down in one of the chairs. Then Star stood as far as she could from Ms. Khan, panting hard.

"Okay, Julian," Ms. Khan said, never taking her eyes off Star. "What was rule number three?"

He remembered right away. "Stay alert, and trust your gut," Julian recited.

"Good," Ms. Khan said. "Now remember—if you

sense that Star is uncomfortable, back up. We're going to start slow. Walk toward us, but stop about ten feet away so she can decide if she wants to get closer."

Julian walked so slowly, it felt unnatural, almost as if he were moving through pudding. Star whipped around to face him. She seemed surprised to see him, like she'd been too freaked out earlier to notice that he was in the room. She watched him approach, the tips of her ears twitching. When he was still several feet away, she shot off in the opposite direction, bumping into one of the empty chairs, sending it clattering against the wall.

"Shoot. I should've put the extra chairs in the office," Bryan said from the other side of the room.

Julian ignored him and kept his attention on Star. She cowered at the end of her leash, her whole body trembling and her tail tucked between her legs.

"It's okay." Julian held out his hand and took a slow step closer. Star's paws scrabbled against the floor as she tried to get farther away. At least she wasn't growling, but Julian could see that she was terrified.

He backed up and tried not to look directly at her.

Star panted, her eyes wild. But as long as Julian didn't move, she stayed put. Julian could feel her fear in his bones. It was hard not to be upset at how scared she was, and part of him wanted to give up. This was going to be much harder than he thought.

But Ms. Khan gave him an encouraging smile. "That was good instinct. Give her a minute to calm down. This will take some time."

Julian stood there, uncertain what to do next.

"Try crouching down," Bryan said softly. "Don't lean over, just kind of squat down so you're more on her level."

Julian glanced at Ms. Khan. She nodded, so he slowly lowered himself.

Bryan kept talking. "People loom over dogs all the time. But we'd be uncomfortable if giants came and stood over us, too!"

To Julian's surprise, it seemed to work. The wild look faded from Star's eyes, and her breathing slowed. He began to feel the tension leave his muscles, too.

He wished he could shrink himself down until he and Star were the same size, so she wouldn't ever have to be afraid of him. He glanced over his shoulder at Bryan. "What next?"

"Have you tried tossing treats to her?" Bryan asked. "Even if she won't take them from your hand, she'll start to think of you as the treat machine."

Julian took a small piece beef jerky from the handful of treats Bryan had given him. He gently lobbed it toward Star. It landed by her left paw. She sniffed it, but didn't pick it up.

Julian wished she could tell him what she wanted. "Why isn't she eating it?" He'd seen the other dogs scarf up these treats, but maybe Star didn't like beef jerky.

"She's just not ready to eat in front of people yet," Ms. Khan said.

"But she'll still associate you with the treat," Bryan added.

The three of them waited. Star sniffed her right paw, as if she didn't even see the treat on her left. She yawned and looked away, like none of them were in the room. Julian didn't know how Bryan and Ms. Khan could be so patient when nothing was happening. He wanted to try a different treat, or at least talk to her. He thought maybe Bryan had another good suggestion, but he and Ms. Khan were just sitting there like statues.

Julian forced himself to follow their lead. Still squatting at Star's level, he took a couple of slow frog steps backwards to give her more space. Then he sat on the floor and stretched out his legs. He looked up at Ms. Khan, and just as he did, Bryan let out a quiet squeal.

"Look! She's eating the treat!" Bryan said.

Julian's head shot around to look at Star. Sure enough, she was chewing. "Try giving her another one now that you're farther away," Bryan said.

Julian tossed another treat. This time, Star kept an eye on him as she gobbled it up. She even took a tiny step closer to him, and Ms. Khan loosened her grip on the leash to give Star some slack. It wasn't much, but it felt like they'd made real progress. And it wouldn't have happened without Bryan's advice.

"That's amazing," Ms. Khan whispered. "I haven't seen her do this for anyone else."

Julian tossed Star a few more treats, and she ate all of them. He was grinning from ear to ear, but he tried to remain as calm as he could so he wouldn't spook Star—or Bryan and Ms. Khan, for that matter.

"That's enough for now," Ms. Khan said, clearly pleased with the results of their work. "We should end on a high note so Star can feel positive about what she did today. You boys head out first, then I'll get her back to her kennel."

With one quick look back over his shoulder, Julian followed Bryan out of the room. He didn't want to see Star panic on the leash again.

They headed out the side door of the shelter and into a small courtyard. Bryan sank onto a stone bench that was surrounded by gold and red fallen leaves. He raked his hands through his curly hair, saying, "That was so cool. I really didn't think she'd ever come around."

"You seem to know a lot about dogs," Julian said.

"Yeah, but that doesn't always matter," Bryan said. "Some dogs only like certain people." He shot Julian a curious look. "And Star seems to really like you."

"I don't think that would've happened without you." As Julian said it, he had a crazy thought, and his next words came out before he could stop himself. "Will you help me train her?"

Bryan's face lit up. "Yes!" he said a little too eagerly.

Julian gulped and smiled back at Bryan weakly. Had he just made a terrible mistake? What was he getting himself into?

Well, whatever it was, Julian hoped it would be worth it for Star.

# ★ CHAPTER 6 ★

**Julian sat at his usual lunch table** at school on Monday, eating the usual turkey and cheese sandwich his dad packed for him in the usual lunch bag. But instead of his mind wandering to maps and adventures far from the school cafeteria, he concentrated on the book about dogs that was splayed on the table beside his sandwich. He'd figured the school library wouldn't have a single book about training a deaf dog, or even any regular dog training books for that matter. The librarian always said she could get books from another school, but Julian couldn't wait that long. He needed to figure out how to train Star *immediately*. So before school that morning, he'd ridden his bike to the main library in town and checked out a book on different dog breeds. If he could figure out what type of dog she was, maybe he'd gain some helpful clues.

He'd flipped through the entire book twice, examining the photos, and determined that Star looked most like an Australian shepherd. The dog in the picture looked just like her, with the same intelligent expression, soft fur, and maplike patches of mottled gray. But the dog in the book didn't have a tail or Star's blue eyes.

The chapter on Australian shepherds was only a few paragraphs long. Julian had hoped to avoid trying to read it in front of other kids, but he couldn't wait until after school to learn more. He tuned out the noise in the cafeteria and ran his finger beneath the words as he slowly read the chapter. He compared the words he was seeing in the description of the dog to the dog's appearance in the photo, which helped him put all the information together. When he was done, he read the chapter again.

The book said that dogs like Star were happiest when they had a job—but what kind of job could a dog have, he wondered. He imagined Star working in an office, like his mom. He chuckled at the thought. She'd be bored enough to eat a computer. He pictured her in nurse's scrubs like his dad, helping patients. The image was so silly that he laughed out loud. A couple of kids at the next table glanced over at him, but he ignored them.

A tray slapped onto the table and — without asking if anyone was sitting there — Bryan dropped into the seat across from him. Now Julian could feel the other kids staring at them.

Bryan leaned over and pulled the dog book toward him. "Hey, that looks just like her," he said in his loud voice. "But I think Star's markings are cooler."

"Me too," Julian said quietly, hoping Bryan would catch the hint. No luck.

"I thought about training her all last night," Bryan announced, just as loudly as before. "I have a plan." His voice always carried across the classroom — and now, across the cafeteria.

Julian could feel the eyes of other kids flitting over them like mosquitoes ready to bite. People already thought he was strange. Being seen with Bryan was *not* going to help.

But Julian couldn't deny that he was curious to hear Bryan's ideas. He'd been trying to come up with a plan himself, but so far he'd drawn a blank. And the suggestions Bryan had come up with on the fly yesterday had really worked. Julian leaned closer as Bryan pulled a folded sheet of paper out of his bag and opened it on the table. On it was a chart, drawn with ruler-straight lines and boxes, each one filled with all kinds of commands and dates for when they'd work on them.

"We'll start with the easy stuff," Bryan said, tapping a finger on a box at the top left corner of the page. "Like *sit* and *lie down*. We'll need roughly two working days for each command."

Julian held back a chuckle at Bryan's seriousness. It was funny, but it was also kind of . . . helpful.

"Then we'll work up to the harder commands," Bryan went on. "You can teach her to give you a high-five or lay her head on her paws or fetch her own leash when it's time to go for a walk."

"Dogs can do all that?" Julian asked. It hadn't even occurred to him that he could teach Star tricks.

"Of course they can," Bryan said matter-of-factly. "The sky's the limit."

Julian held back another laugh. He studied the chart, the boxes like a grid. If he could get through each one, his parents would have to trust him—and let him adopt Star. But it seemed impossible, not only because he'd never trained a dog, but because Star wasn't exactly the perfect student. "Um—Bryan?"

"Yes, Julian?" Bryan said, like a teacher calling on a student.

"How do we teach her all of this when she won't even let us touch her?"

"Not to worry." Bryan took a big bite of greasy pepperoni pizza. "I've helped train lots of dogs. I'll show you how it's done."

Talking with his mouth full and gesturing wildly, Bryan started to explain how he used treats to get certain dogs to learn commands, but other dogs liked toys better than treats. Julian glanced around the cafeteria, worried that everyone was watching Bryan's enthusiastic hand movements as he described different training methods. At one point he stood up and imitated a dog learning to move from a down position up to a sitting position.

"Maybe we should talk about this later," Julian said, beckoning Bryan back to his seat.

"Why?" Bryan said from a half squat.

"People are staring." Julian picked at the crust of his sandwich, embarrassed that Bryan didn't even seem to notice how much of a scene he was making.

With a shake of his head, Bryan sat down again. He leaned in and lowered his voice. "You care about Star, right?"

"Of course!" Julian said. "All I've been able to think about is how to help her."

"When something is this important, I tune everyone out," Bryan said. "I know they might be judging me, but I can't let that distract me from what really matters."

He said it as though it was the simplest thing in the world, but Julian wasn't so sure it would be that easy for him. He couldn't imagine just tuning out what other people thought of him. Still, for Star's sake, he was willing to try. He stole a glance toward the tables around them. All the other students had turned back to their own lunches and conversations.

Julian took a bite of his sandwich. "Tell me more about what kind of treats you use."

When Julian and Bryan arrived at the shelter after school, Ms. Khan continued the training that they'd started the day before. They worked with Star for a while, and then she brought a puppy named Bumble outside to demonstrate some basic dog-handling techniques. Bumble was a friendly, happy six-month-old who loved attention and already knew the *sit* command. Julian couldn't believe how much easier it was to work with her than with Star.

They worked with a few different dogs as Ms. Khan showed them how to approach a dog in the kennel, clip on the leash, and walk outside. Julian loved learning how to handle the different animals and getting to pet them, but he couldn't wait until it was time to work with Star.

Finally Ms. Khan sent the boys to the socialization room while she got Star. Julian and Bryan sat in the chairs to wait. A couple minutes later Star pulled Ms. Khan through the door. The dog's ears were pinned back and her eyes darted around the room, but she didn't seem *quite* as freaked out as she had been the day before. Maybe she was even starting to like being out of her kennel, Julian thought.

Julian and Bryan sat quietly while Ms. Khan let Star sniff around the room. Once Star had settled down enough to stop pacing and panting, Ms. Khan said, "Come take the leash from me, Julian. Let's see how she does when it's just the two of you."

"You're leaving?" Julian's heart jumped into his throat. As excited as he was about working with Star, he wasn't sure he was ready to do it on his own. The squares of Bryan's training chart swam around in his head.

"Nope. I'm just handing over the reins." Ms. Khan passed the loop handle of the leash to Julian, then sat down in one of the chairs. He held tight to the faded red strip of nylon connecting him to Star. Star tilted her head, as if asking him what they should do now. Julian swallowed hard. He had absolutely no idea.

"Hey, Star," he said, before remembering that she couldn't hear him say hello and giving her a small wave. He felt silly waving at a dog, but she watched his hand, then looked at his face. He crouched down. She waited a second, then slunk toward him. She stopped a few feet away, but she was close enough that Julian could reach out and pet her if he wanted to. He did want to, but he knew he had to take it slow. It had never worked when people tried to rush him, so he made a silent promise to let Star set her own pace.

"Why don't you see if she'll follow you a few steps," Bryan suggested. "Maybe you can get her used to the leash."

Ms. Khan nodded. "Good idea."

"Okay." Julian slowly stood and took a step back. Star didn't freak out, but she didn't follow him either. He tried to encourage her. "Come on, Star."

She didn't move.

Julian took another step, the leash stretching taut between them. As soon as there was no more slack,

Star felt the light tug of the leash on her collar and panicked. She jerked backwards and started whipping her head back and forth, trying to get away from the leash. But her frantic movements only made it pull harder on her collar, which tightened around her throat. She leaped into the air and pawed and snapped at the nylon, letting out a high-pitched scream unlike any noise Julian had ever heard.

Star's terrified energy filled the room. Julian could practically feel the weight of her fear. His eyes went wide as her desperate movements yanked his arm back and forth. "What do I do?"

"Drop the leash!" Ms. Khan said.

Julian let go. As soon as the leash was no longer pulling on her, Star retreated to a corner of the room, panting hard. Ms. Khan was on her feet, standing between Star and the boys. "Is everyone okay?"

"We're fine," Bryan said. "Star just got scared."

Julian felt out of breath, too. "She acted like it was attacking her."

"Before she got here, she didn't know what a leash was," Ms. Khan said, studying Julian carefully. Star shook out her whole body, from her ears to her tail, as if she could shake off her fear.

Julian tried to imagine what Star thought of the leash snaking from her collar. If he was in a strange place and someone tried to lead him around with no explanation, he'd probably freak out, too. But the concern on Ms. Khan's face made him scared that he'd messed up and he wouldn't be allowed to work with Star anymore. "Can I still train her?"

Ms. Khan looked from Star to the boys and back again, as if she were trying to make a difficult decision. Julian held his breath. The dog sat in the corner, watching them, her breathing slowing to a normal pace. "Tell you what," Ms. Khan said after a long moment. "Let's try some things without touching the leash. Just let her drag it on the floor."

Julian exhaled with relief. "What kind of things—"

"The training plan," Bryan interrupted. "We can still use it."

"Training plan, huh, Bryan?" Ms. Khan grinned. She didn't sound surprised, and Julian guessed this wasn't the first time Bryan had shared one of his highly detailed ideas with her. Bryan took the paper out of his pocket. He unfolded the sheet and started to explain every step to Ms. Khan.

Since Julian had already heard the whole thing at lunch, he turned to Star. He took a half step closer to her. She pressed her back into the corner, her fur against the wall. But she wasn't trembling, Julian noticed. He tossed her a treat. She stretched out her snout and sniffed it, hesitating for a second. Then she gently nipped at it with her front teeth, pulled it into her mouth, and chomped it down. Licking her chops, she looked up at him expectantly, which made Julian feel better. Maybe she'd forgiven him for the leash.

"That's a pretty good plan," Ms. Khan said when Bryan had finished his speech. Just then, the phone started ringing in her office, making them all jump.

"I better get that." Ms. Khan hesitated, then looked from Star to the boys. "You good?"

Julian and Bryan nodded.

"I'll be right in there if you need me." She hurried into the office and closed the door partway behind her as she answered the phone.

Julian glanced at Star, hoping she wouldn't freak out again. She was looking pretty calm, but she was still pressed into the corner like she was glued to it. "Okay, Bryan. Where do we start?"

Bryan tapped the paper in his hand. "At the beginning. The first command is *sit*."

"How do I teach her to sit when she's already sitting?" Julian asked.

"Simple. Put a treat by her nose to get her to stand up, then when she's standing, slowly move the treat over her head so she has to look up." Bryan demonstrated the move as if there were an invisible dog in front him. "She'll automatically put her rump down as her head comes up, and you'll tell her to sit, so she learns the command."

"Buuuuut . . ." Bryan sounded so confident that Julian hated having to ask the question. "How exactly will she know what I'm saying?" he asked.

Bryan blinked at him, then smacked his palm against his forehead. "Oh, right. Of course. Um, well, she'll follow the treat. It'll still make sense to her."

For the first time Julian could remember, Bryan sounded slightly unsure of himself.

"Okay, I'll give it a try." Julian stepped toward Star with the treat in his outstretched hand. But she wasn't looking at him. She had turned her attention to the leash that hung over her shoulder and lay in a pile by her feet. She startled when Julian got too close, and she scuttled sideways along the wall.

"Try putting the treat right by her nose so she knows you have it," Bryan suggested.

Julian crouched down and stretched his arm until the treat was within a couple inches of Star's face. Her nose twitched, but she didn't take it.

"What now?" Frustration was building inside him like a volcano. His palms started to sweat and his heart was beating faster. He should just give up now. This was one more thing he wasn't going to be able to do. His parents could just tell him he wasn't responsible enough. And Bryan and Ms. Khan could be disappointed in him, like everyone else.

"Maybe she'd like a toy," Bryan suggested. He

dug through the basket of toys in search of the perfect one. Julian wasn't sure why the knotted ropes and rubber bones Bryan rejected weren't good enough, but he turned his attention back to Star. Her gaze flicked from him to Bryan to the half-open door of the office. Ms. Khan had hung up the phone, but she stayed in the office, tapping at her keyboard. Star looked worried, but at least she wasn't panicking anymore.

Julian couldn't let Star down. If treats and toys weren't going to work, he had to find a different way to gain her trust. He took a deep breath and forced himself to think about how he'd gotten through to her before. He'd just . . . sat still in front of her cage. That was it! Maybe he needed to spend time with her without asking her to do anything, so she knew she could trust him.

Julian sank to his knees. He sneaked glances at Star, careful not to stare at her. He tossed her another treat, but she ignored it.

Bryan finally looked up from the basket with a triumphant expression on his face and a stuffed dog toy that looked like a trout in his hand. He nodded when he saw Julian on the floor. "Great thinking. She needs to get used to us."

Bryan got down on all fours, crawled toward Julian and Star, stopped a few feet away, and slid the stuffed fish the rest of the way. Then he plopped down cross-legged on the floor. Julian watched Star watching Bryan and almost burst out laughing. She had a confused expression on her face, as if Bryan were the strangest dog she'd ever seen.

But Bryan didn't seem to mind. He was too busy formulating a new plan. "Sometimes it helps just to sit and pretend the dog isn't even there," he said without looking at Star. "We should just talk and let her come to us."

"Um, okay." Julian shifted so he was sitting cross-legged on the floor, too, facing Bryan. "So, how do you know so much about dogs?"

Bryan rubbed at a spot of dirt on the side of his shoe. He kept his eyes down while he spoke. "I had a hard time at my last school. I . . . I didn't really have a lot of friends. My dad started taking me to the shelter in my old town to volunteer because I love being around dogs.

Dogs are the best. They don't judge you or tease you. So I decided to learn as much about them as I could, and when we moved here, I started coming to this shelter."

Something in Bryan's voice felt familiar to Julian. He certainly knew what it was like to have a hard time at school, and he felt bad that it had taken him so long to give Bryan a chance. "That's really cool."

"Thanks." Bryan shot Star a sideways glance. "I like being able to help them."

"Does the shelter get a lot of dogs like Star?" Julian asked.

"No way!" Bryan looked up at Julian. "I mean, sometimes we get dogs who are a little scared, like Pip, but I haven't seen any other deaf dogs since I moved here. Ms. Khan says they come in sometimes. But no one else is like Star."

"You mean because she's so difficult?" Julian knew he was supposed to be ignoring Star, but he tossed her a treat just in case she somehow understood what he was saying.

Bryan shook his head. "Because she's so special."

Julian grinned. "I thought it was just me, because I

haven't spent a lot of time around dogs. There's something about her, right?"

"You can tell how smart she is," Bryan agreed. "She's just . . . different."

Out of the corner of his eye, Julian saw Star tip her head to the side, almost as if she were following their conversation. He could've sworn she'd moved a little closer when he wasn't paying attention.

"I get it," Julian said, looking at the ground and swallowing the lump in his throat. "I'm different, too." He'd never admitted this to anyone. He glanced self-consciously at the office door and lowered his voice, hoping Ms. Khan wasn't listening. "I have dyslexia, so school is really hard. Most of the time I feel like I'm not good at anything."

Bryan let out a snort of laughter. Julian's head shot up, and he glared at him. What kind of response was that? Maybe his first impression of Bryan had been right all along. He instantly regretted saying anything —this was why he should just keep to himself.

"No way!" Bryan blurted out, his face lit up by a giant smile.

Julian had never seen anyone so excited about his diagnosis. Usually when people heard about it, they looked away and shifted from foot to foot and got all uncomfortable. They never really knew what it meant, but they did understand that it made Julian different. The worst was that when people found out, they treated him like he was stupid. There was basically no good response, which was why Julian had decided long ago to stop talking about it.

But Bryan's reaction—that was a new low. No one had ever outright *laughed* at him.

Bryan must have seen the shocked look on Julian's face, because he held up both hands and shook his head. "What I mean is—I have dyslexia too!"

Julian's jaw dropped. "You do? Seriously? Or are you messing with me? Because—"

"I'm serious! Me too!" Bryan was grinning at him again. He almost made it seem like dyslexia was some cool thing they had in common.

Julian thought about it for a second. He *did* like the idea of knowing someone else who understood what he was going through. But how could Bryan have dyslexia? He was such a brainiac! "But you do so well at school," Julian said. "And you're always reading."

"Sure, but that doesn't mean it's easy for me. I have to work extra hard," Bryan said. "I have to read all the time to keep practicing, and I wear headphones to tune out distractions." He shrugged. "I know other kids think I'm weird. But I did a bunch of research, and I found out that lots of famous people had dyslexia. Even Einstein!"

"Really? How is that possible?" Julian asked.

"Our brains function differently from everyone else's. It's like a superpower." Bryan started gesturing as he explained. Star followed his movements with her eyes. "Yes, sure—it's harder to decode language. But the same thing in our brains that makes reading so hard makes us really good at other stuff. I'm great at art and inventing things. Right now, it's mostly little things, but maybe one day I'll work with robots."

Julian was shocked. He had never known that being dyslexic could be an actual advantage for some things. He tried to think of what he was really good at, and he could come up with only one thing: maps.

It had never occurred to him that his dyslexia might be the reason he was so good at remembering landscapes and directions and every corner he turned. It might even explain his love of maps and drawing.

Maybe, Julian thought, he could even be the Einstein of maps someday! After all those years of struggling and feeling like he was doing everything all wrong all the time, something in his brain clicked. He started to see himself in a different way.

Julian felt a little guilty for having thought that Bryan was weird. He was actually pretty cool, and they had more in common than he'd ever imagined.

Bryan's eyes went wide. "Don't look now, but someone is really close to you."

While they'd been talking, Star had quietly moved close enough to sniff Julian, her cold nose tickling his arm. He held his breath, not wanting to scare her away. She sniffed at the fish-shaped toy in his hand. Julian wondered if dog toys were as unfamiliar to her as the leash.

He reached toward Star in slow motion, as if he were moving through thick mud. With just the tips of his fingers, he lightly touched one of the gray patches on her back. Her fur was the softest thing he'd ever felt, softer than his mom's favorite fleece throw blanket. Amazingly, Star let him pet her.

She inched even closer and stood right next to Julian, then sniffed in Bryan's direction. Bryan held out his hand, and she nosed his palm.

A huge smile spread across Bryan's face. "She's never gotten this close to me before."

Julian was grinning like a little kid too. He felt like he was floating as he ran his fingers through the dog's silky fur. Star was finally beginning to trust him. She might not be ready for the leash right away—maybe not for a long time—but Julian didn't care. For the first time he could remember, he felt like he had actually succeeded at something. And along the way, he'd found not one but two new friends.

# ★ CHAPTER 7 ★

**Julian kept replaying** in his mind his last training session with Star. Well, it couldn't exactly be called training. He hadn't taught her to do anything except touch his hand with her nose to get a treat. But she was coming right up to him when he walked into the socialization room, and that was huge. She leaned into him as he petted her, and she took treats right from his hand. She was so gentle, her mouth barely brushing the tips of his fingers before she scarfed down the snacks. Now he just had to figure out how to actually train her. He didn't know how she'd ever learn commands without being able to hear what he was saying.

"Julian!" His mom's voice snapped him out of his daydream. "Come on, we've got three more questions. What is the main theme of this chapter?"

Julian thumbed through the book, searching for clues. He'd actually managed to make it through the whole chapter with his parents, but his mind had been so full of thoughts of Star that he could barely remember what he'd read. A few familiar words jumped out at him—parents, brother, child. He took a wild guess. "Is the theme family?"

"Try again," his mom encouraged. "Think about what you read."

If only it were that easy. By the time he decoded the words, it was hard to keep track of what they were actually saying.

"Love?" Julian guessed. Weren't most books about love in the end?

His mom sighed. "No. It's about individuality and choice."

Julian let the book fall to the table and covered his face with his hands. If he had a choice, he'd be at the shelter with Star instead of doing homework. At this rate, he'd never manage to get through it all before his parents gave up.

"Are you sure the theme isn't time?" Henry said, ruffling the back of Julian's head as he walked out of the pantry with a box of crackers in his hand. "This is taking forever."

Julian swatted his brother's hand away. Everything was so simple for him.

"Henry, what are you doing?" their dad said. "We're going to your grandfather's house for dinner."

"I'm starving. And it'll be hours before we go if we have to wait for Jules to finish his homework."

"Be nice to your brother," his dad warned.

Julian's mom pushed her chair back. "Look at the time! We're late for Grandpa's birthday dinner." She set Julian's assignment on the table. "We'll have to finish later, Jules."

Julian felt a rush of relief. He jumped up from the table and grabbed the baking dish off the counter, leaving his homework behind.

When they finally pulled up to Grandpa's house,

an exasperated Aunt Carol opened the door. "There you are! We were about to give up on you."

Julian felt his cheeks turn pink. He looked at his mom, dad, and brother, but no one admitted that it was his fault that they were late. They stepped into the house, which was warm and full of food smells and noisy with conversation. Julian looked through the sliding glass door to the backyard and saw his cousins chasing one another around on the grass. Julian's mom had three sisters and two brothers, and they'd all brought their families over for Grandpa's big birthday.

The entire dining room table was teeming with foil-covered casseroles and serving bowls full of salad. Aunt Sharon shuffled the dishes around so Julian could add his dad's Mexican lasagna to the spread. His grandpa laid a hand on his shoulder. "You brought my favorite!"

Julian gave his grandpa a hug, careful not to bump against his cane. "Happy birthday, Grandpa."

"Let's eat," his grandpa said, picking up a plate and handing it to him. "Fill 'er up for me, would you, kid?" Julian piled the plate high with food and carried it to one of the tables that were set up on the back patio. He got his grandpa settled in a chair, then went back for his own dinner. No one in his family had to be told twice to eat, so Julian had to wait for his cousins, aunts, and uncles to finish getting their food before he could get close to the buffet again.

All of Julian's cousins were either little kids or off at college, so he never had anyone his own age to talk to at family gatherings. Well, he did have Henry, but Julian tried to steer clear of him. He wasn't in the mood for any more teasing.

While he waited for the buffet line to move, Julian glanced at the picture frames crowding the mantel. Among all the old wedding and school photos was a black-and-white picture of Grandpa, young and trim in his army uniform, with a German shepherd sitting proudly by his side. This had always been Julian's favorite photo. He loved the stories of all the adventures his grandfather had with his dog, Liberty. Finally it was his turn to get dinner, and as he loaded his plate with food, he imagined himself and Star having their own adventures.

It was getting dark by the time the family sang "Happy Birthday." Julian's mom cut the cake, and dinner plates were stacked and carried into the kitchen to be replaced by dessert plates. Someone turned on the lights that were strung above the patio and lit the vanilla-scented candles on the table. The little kids had taken their cake inside to play with Grandpa's old board games. Julian was getting restless. He still had to finish his homework, and he wanted to watch more dog training videos before going back to the shelter tomorrow. But he knew it would be a while before the party wound down.

Grandpa set down a plate heavy with chocolate cake and strawberry ice cream next to Julian at the end of the table. "You've been quiet tonight. What are you making there, kid?"

Julian had been drawing designs in his frosting with the tip of his fork. He suddenly realized that he'd been drawing Star. "It's a dog I've been trying to help at the shelter. Her name is Star. But she's deaf, so I don't know how to talk to her."

Grandpa took a bite of cake. "You know, I had a dog once. Back in the military."

"Liberty, right?" Julian thought of the photo on the mantel.

"That was my girl." Grandpa smiled sadly.

"I bet she was a really good dog," Julian said.

"She was the best." Grandpa leaned closer and lowered his voice. "And I'll let you in on a secret. You don't need words to talk to your dog. We trained our dogs using hand signals."

Julian perked up. "You did?"

Grandpa nodded. "It was a good way to bond with them. But more importantly, we had to be able to give them commands without speaking, in case we were ever in a dangerous situation and couldn't make a sound."

Julian imagined his grandpa signing to Liberty to stay still while enemy soldiers patrolled nearby—and the dog knowing exactly what he wanted. It made sense. Dogs had to learn English, so why not hand signals?

"Can you teach me?" he asked eagerly.

"Sure. Soon as we're done with our cake." Grandpa winked at Julian as he shoved a big forkful of dessert into his mouth. Julian knew that his mom was trying to get Grandpa to eat healthier, but she had to give in to his sweet tooth on his birthday. Julian smiled and took a bite of his own cake.

"Did I ever tell you about the first time I met Liberty?" Grandpa asked. Julian shook his head. He'd heard about the time Grandpa carried Liberty across a swamp on his shoulders and the time Liberty stole a candy bar for him from a friend's bunk. But he never knew how they first met.

"Well, I knew from the beginning that I wanted to be part of a K-9 team. I did everything possible to get into the program. I must have washed a thousand dog bowls before they finally put me in training. I trained with a dog named Bear. Took care of him day and night, learned all the commands he knew. But at the end of training, Bear was up for retirement. After all that work, I was left without a dog." Grandpa paused to take another bite. "Then, two days later, I saw the kennel master out with the prettiest shepherd I'd ever seen. Beautiful, but stubborn."

"Liberty?" Julian guessed.

Grandpa nodded. "She was supposed be climbing over a wall. But when I walked up to the training yard, she ignored the wall and came straight for the fence. She climbed right over and into my arms. The kennel master had just about had it with her and was ready to ship her off to civilian life. But I saw something in her. I knew she was special. He gave me three days to get her through the whole obstacle course, and we did it."

"How?" Julian asked.

"Most people think dog training is about getting the dog to listen to you. But most of the time it's about listening to your dog. Liberty just needed someone who understood her." Grandpa scraped the last bit of frosting off his plate, licked his fork clean, and stood up. "Come on. I'll show you some of her hand signals."

Julian helped Grandpa down the three steps from the patio to the lawn. It was a cool fall night, and Uncle Daniel had started a fire in the fire pit. Julian saw Henry and his dad among the small cluster of adults huddled around the crackling flames. Most of the family had gone inside, so the yard was pretty quiet.

Grandpa led Julian across the grass, away from the others. "You have to remember that dogs notice everything. So you don't have to wave your arms around like you're signaling an airplane. Your signals can be small, but keep them consistent. Especially with your dog—she may not be able to hear, but you can be sure she's watching you."

"Got it." Julian liked the way Grandpa referred to Star as his dog.

Grandpa nodded, satisfied that Julian was taking in the lesson. Then he stood tall and proud, as if he were back in uniform, his arms hanging at his sides. Then he raised his right arm and held it straight out in front of him, parallel to the ground, with his open palm facing the sky. "That means *sit*. Give it a try."

Julian straightened his back, trying to stand like a soldier. He swept his arm forward from his side, with his palm up.

"Good," Grandpa said. "Now, to get your dog to lie down, point your hand toward the ground." He turned his palm face-down. Keeping his arm straight and his hand flat, he lowered his arm until his fingers pointed at the grass. Julian copied his movement. They repeated the two commands over and over as Grandpa told Julian more stories about Liberty.

Julian could picture Star responding to the commands, like they had their own secret language. An idea popped into his head. "If I can teach her hand signals for all these different commands, can I teach her one for her name? That way she'll know when I'm talking to her?"

"Sure can. You said her name was Star, right?"

Julian nodded.

Grandpa thought about it for a moment. Then he spread out his fingers and waggled them gently, making a small wave motion. "How about this? Like a glimmering star."

Julian remembered how Star had watched his hand when he'd waved at her, as if she'd known it was just for her. He brightened. "That's perfect. Thanks, Grandpa!"

Julian's mom stepped out onto the patio. "What are you two up to out here?"

"Grandpa's teaching me how to train dogs," Julian said. "So I can work with them at the shelter."

His mom seemed a little surprised. "You're really dedicated to those dogs, aren't you?" she said.

"He sure is," Grandpa said. Julian nodded in agreement. He wanted to prove to both of them that he could do this.

To Julian's astonishment, his mom smiled. "I'll leave you to it, then." And without another word, she turned back toward the house.

"There's one more you need to know," Grandpa said.

"What's that?" Julian's mind was whirring as he tried to soak up everything his grandpa had told him.

Grandpa flashed him a thumbs-up.

"Okay," Julian said. "What's the last command?"

"That's it." Grandpa gave him another thumbs-up. "You can't tell her with words that she's a good dog, so you need a sign to tell her she got it right."

Julian stuck his own thumb in the air uncertainly. Then he dropped his hands to his sides. "This will really work?"

"Of course it will." Grandpa put his arm around Julian's shoulder. "Training will help you build trust so she knows you're part of the same pack. But the most important thing is that you're there for her and you care. Once she knows she can rely on you, she'll come around."

Julian squared his shoulders as he stood beside his grandpa. He was starting to understand his purpose now. He was going to communicate with Star. And he knew exactly how.

# ★ CHAPTER 8 ★

**Julian and Bryan** headed to the shelter together after school. When they got there, Bryan pulled a sandwich bag full of shredded chicken out of his backpack. "I thought we should give Star something really special for her training. This should get her attention."

"She'll like that. I brought something, too." Julian handed Bryan a folded stack of paper.

"What is this?" Bryan asked, unfolding the pages.

"My grandpa trained dogs in the army. He showed me some of the hand signals they used so they could give their dogs commands when they had to stay quiet in enemy territory. I found even more online." Julian had stayed up late watching videos on dog training websites and carefully drawing each signal so he'd remember them. He'd even drawn himself giving the signals to Star in different scenes. On the page, she was sitting in a field, lying down in his room, and staying on the steps of the Winderhouser porch.

"Cool!" Bryan traced his finger along the drawings as they headed inside. "This is like a comic book. You and Star are dog training superheroes."

Julian hesitated in the hallway. He turned back to Bryan. "She has to be looking at me for the signals to work. But I don't know how to get her attention if she's distracted. What if she's sniffing a tree or something and I want her to sit?"

"How did your Grandpa do it?"

"I don't know," Julian admitted. "I didn't think to ask. I was just trying to learn the signals."

Bryan ran a hand through his curls and narrowed his eyes.

"What if you stomped your feet so she could feel the vibration?" Bryan said.

"I'm not an elephant," Julian said. "How do I stomp hard enough to shake the ground?"

"Good point. That might only work on old floors." Bryan squinted again. "What about flashing a light or something?"

Ms. Khan came around the corner carrying a stack of towels almost as tall as she was. "What are you two talking about?"

"How to get Star's attention since we can't call her name," Bryan said.

"I've got just the thing." Ms. Khan nodded for them to follow her. The boys helped carry the towels to the linen closet, then trailed her to the office. On her desk was a black plastic collar with a small rectangular box—about three inches wide—attached to it. "This is a vibration collar. I got it just for Star, but since she wouldn't let us get close, I couldn't put it on her. I've seen how good she is with you, though. I bet she'll let you do it."

"Will it hurt her?" Julian asked.

"Not at all. It's just enough to get her attention."

Ms. Khan placed the box against her arm and picked up a small remote control. She pushed the button, and Julian heard a faint buzzing sound coming from the box. "See? No pain. Want to give it a try?"

The boys took turns pressing the collar against their own arms. It tickled Julian's skin, but Ms. Khan was right—it didn't hurt. She showed them how to use the remote control, then handed the whole set over to Julian. She also gave him a brand-new purple nylon collar. "While you're at it, see if you can get this on her, too."

"Why does she need a new collar?" Julian wondered if Star would be sad to lose her last connection to Mrs. Winderhouser.

"The one she's got on is going to fall apart any day now. Plus this one's got a tag for the shelter instead of her old owner's information," Ms. Khan said. "That way, if she ever gets lost, people will know to call us."

Julian gripped the purple collar tightly. This was one assignment he was determined to complete.

• • •

Julian hid the collars under the dog bed in the socialization room. He didn't want Star to see them until he was sure she was ready. He remembered what his grandpa had said about building trust.

Ms. Khan brought Star into the room from her kennel. Star still pulled and panted, her claws scratching against the floor until Ms. Khan dropped the leash. But she wasn't leaping around or trying to get away. She settled into her corner, and Ms. Khan, with a final nod at the boys, headed for the office so they could put their training plan into action.

Julian wanted to start by teaching Star the thumbs-up signal. The dog watched his legs as he moved closer to her, and she studied his face as he got on his knees about three feet away. They were at the same eye level, and she lifted her nose toward him, probably to smell where he'd been and what he'd had for lunch. He gave her a thumbs-up for looking at him and tossed her a piece of chicken. Her blue eyes went wide, as if she'd won a raffle. The chicken was gone in a flash. She looked at him again, her ears perked up, as if asking whether there was more where that came from. Julian grinned. Star got another thumbs-up and another treat.

"Good girl." He scooted closer. Star didn't cower at all. Julian gave her a thumbs-up, but this time, instead of tossing the piece of chicken, he held it out toward her. She scooted forward and took the treat right from his hand. Julian wanted to leap for joy.

"Yes!" Bryan said. "That was huge. Now try teaching her to sit."

"Okay." Julian closed his eyes for a second, picturing the hand signal he'd drawn and remembering how his grandpa had raised his arm, palm up, in a single smooth motion. When he opened his eyes, Star was watching him, her head tilted to the side, as if she were waiting for the next signal.

Julian held a treat between his fingers with his palm facing up. He put it right by her nose, then lifted his hand before she could grab it. Her nose followed the chicken, and she sat. Julian was so surprised, he almost forgot to give her the reward. He quickly gave her a thumbs-up and handed her the treat. He tried it again and again to make sure it hadn't just been luck. Star got it right every time.

"You're such a smart girl!" Julian scratched her behind the ears. She leaned against his hand and stepped closer, placing her paw on Julian's shoe. And for the first time, she wagged her tail.

"Did you see that?" Julian asked.

"Whoa," Bryan said in an awestruck whisper. "She's like a new dog."

"Then maybe it's time for her to get a new collar."

Bryan passed him the purple collar. Julian held it out so Star could sniff it. "What do you think?"

She nosed the collar, sniffing every inch of it. When she was done, she looked up at Julian. He gave her a thumbs-up and another treat, then let her lick the chicken off his fingers. He was afraid she might freak out when he touched her old collar, the way she did when he'd tried to walk her on the leash. He handed her another treat, and as she gently nipped it from his fingers, he touched the grimy collar around her neck. She stayed calm. As quickly and gently as he could, he unclipped the old collar and snapped on the new one.

"Well done!" Bryan cheered him on.

Julian tucked the old collar in his back pocket so Star couldn't see it and took the vibration collar from Bryan. He held out another piece of chicken, and Star let him put the second collar on her, too. He scratched her behind the ear. She rubbed her head against his hand. "You look good in purple," he said.

Julian practiced the *sit* command with Star a couple more times. She was totally focused on him, her blue eyes fixed on his every movement. Julian wanted to try the vibration collar to see if it would get her attention. He had the remote in one hand and the treats in the other. He pressed the button for half a second and immediately gave Star a treat. She barely seemed to notice. "Do you think it worked?" he asked Bryan.

"I don't know," Bryan said. "Maybe she blinked?"

Julian wanted to get Star to look somewhere else so he could try to get her attention, but she wouldn't take her eyes off him. "See if you can get her to watch you," Julian said to Bryan.

Bryan started hopping from one foot to the other

in front of the door, his curls bouncing. Julian couldn't help laughing as Bryan danced around—if you could call it that. But it got Star's attention. The dog watched Bryan, her face full of curiosity. Julian was pretty sure that if she were a person, she'd be cracking up, too.

This was his chance. Julian pushed the button on the remote, and Star's head whipped around to face him. It had worked! He quickly gave her a treat, then realized he'd forgotten to give her a thumbs-up, so he gave the signal and another treat. Her tail swished back and forth.

"I think she gets it," Julian said.

"Can I stop dancing now?" Bryan asked.

Julian laughed. "Yeah. I think we can all take a break."

Bryan dropped into one of the chairs. Julian sat on the floor by the dog bed. He took the stuffed trout out of the basket and passed it back and forth between his hands. "I can't believe that actually worked. The sitting, the collar, everything!"

"Dogs don't miss anything," Bryan said. "Even

though she was playing it cool, she totally knew what you were up to. She *let* you put the collars on her. She really trusts you."

"The chicken helped a lot," Julian said.

Bryan grinned. "Don't tell my mom I fed her left-overs to the dogs."

"Seriously?" Julian's eyes went wide. He tried to imagine sneaking food from his plate to bring to the shelter. His parents were so wiped out by dinner that they probably wouldn't notice, but with his luck, Henry would catch him.

"It was worth it," Bryan said. "When Star wagged her tail? I was starting to think her tail didn't work right. All she'd ever done was tuck it under her belly."

"That was awesome," Julian said. They'd made so much progress, and he was glad he had someone to share this with.

As the boys talked, Star crawled onto the dog bed and curled up beside Julian. He ran his fingers through her soft fur and traced the map of gray patches on her back. Her breathing slowed beneath his hand, and soon her eyes closed. She fell asleep, relaxed and content, her back warm against Julian's leg. His chest swelled with pride. For the first time, she really felt like his dog.

# ★ CHAPTER 9 ★

**Julian sat at a table** in the school library with an atlas and a history book about Michigan spread out in front of him. As he read, he flipped Star's old tag back and forth in his hand, running his thumb over the engraved numbers, 11-25-15. It felt like a good luck charm. He'd asked Ms. Khan if he could keep the tag when he'd turned in Star's old collar.

"Of course!" she had said. "Great job today." He'd tucked the tag into his pocket. And now he kept it there to remind himself, whenever he got frustrated at school or home, of how well the training was going.

Julian and the rest of his class were in the library to look up facts on the empires of the Western Hemisphere so they could fill out a work sheet. Anyway, that's what he was supposed to be doing. Julian had started to do the assignment, but he'd gotten lost in a map of the Roman Empire. Then he'd started thinking about how the Romans must have left behind all sorts of buried treasure, so he looked for books about that. The library didn't have any, but that's when he remembered a book he'd checked out once that had a chapter on buried treasure right there in Michigan.

Julian and Henry used to make up all kinds of adventure games when they were little, before Henry started teasing him about school. They'd play pirates or cops and robbers. They'd pretend to be soldiers sneaking through the woods or bandits who needed to escape across the lake. When he got older, Julian learned that the Great Lakes had been such a busy trade route that there really had been pirates and bank robbers—and shipwrecks and shootouts—there. And they'd left all kinds of gold and silver sunk in the lakes and buried in the fields—just like old movies about the Wild West, except in his own backyard.

Bryan flopped into the seat next to him. "What are you reading?"

Julian wanted to shuffle the books under his notebook. He didn't want Bryan to make fun of him for looking for treasure, but he wasn't fast enough. Bryan pulled the history book toward him, and his face lit up. He leaned in and whispered, "Have you gotten to the chapter on shipwrecks?"

Julian's eyes went wide with surprise. Bryan liked this book, too? "Not yet."

"There are all these shipwrecks sitting out there in the lakes," Bryan said, his voice rising with excitement. "Just like the ones you see in pirate movies. And no one really knows what's in them all. Some of them could have millions of dollars in gold."

"My grandpa said there are supposed to be thousands of wrecks out there," Julian said. He wished he'd been able to read all the placards at the shipwreck exhibit they'd gone to at the museum. His grandpa would have helped him, but with other people around, Julian had been too embarrassed to stand there struggling through all the words. Instead, he had spent the day studying the old maps and artifacts that were rusted by lake water.

"More than six thousand!" Bryan said, lowering his voice as if he were sharing a big secret. "I started reading up on it before I moved here. I couldn't picture *lakes* with pirates and shipwrecks. The only lakes I ever saw were flat and calm. I had no idea how big and stormy the Great Lakes were. Or how much cash was shipped on boats."

As soon as Bryan paused to take a breath, Julian jumped in. "There's buried treasure all over Michigan. Not just in the lakes."

"I read about that, too!" Bryan said. "All these loggers would hide their gold in the middle of the woods, and farmers buried everything in their fields—back before everyone used banks. How come no one ever talks about how wild it was out here?"

Julian was amazed at how much Bryan had read. He seemed to know everything. He wondered how Bryan did it with his dyslexia, but Julian was too caught up in finally having someone as interested in buried treasure as he was to ask about it. He never would have imagined that Bryan was curious about all these things. Julian had been wrong about the new kid, just like everyone else had been too.

"Did you hear about the people who stole money from banks in Chicago?" Julian asked. "During the big fire. They brought it here to hide it."

"No way!" Bryan said. "Why haven't they made a movie about that?"

Julian smiled, happy to be able to teach Bryan something for a change. He rummaged in his backpack until he found one of his old maps of the Lake Michigan coast, and he carefully unfolded the crackling, yellowed paper and laid it on the table. He'd never shown anyone else at school his maps, but he didn't feel self-conscious around Bryan. He could imagine them mapping out an adventure together, searching for treasure.

"Lots of the treasures are still out there," Julian said. "Or at least no one knows for sure if they've been found." He pointed to a few markings along the coast. "These used to be old hunting camps. I wouldn't be surprised if some of the money is buried in one of these places. No one knows exactly where, because the land has changed so much. But these old maps have all kinds of clues."

Bryan leaned over the faded paper, studying it with narrowed eyes. "I bet you're right. Where did you find this?"

"I've got a ton of them," Julian said. "My dad and I find them at garage sales." Julian's parents had figured out how good he was with maps when their GPS stopped working on a family road trip. Using an old map from the glove compartment, he'd navigated them across the Upper Peninsula to their campsite in the Porcupine Mountains. Ever since then, his parents had helped him build his map collection. His favorites were the antique ones with forgotten territories, logging roads, and railroad tracks.

"I love old maps," Bryan said. "It's like they're full of secrets right under our feet. I've got one that's like a hundred years old—from a gold rush camp out in California."

"That's really cool." Julian had never met anyone who cared about old maps and treasure hunting as much as he did. He flipped the pages of the history book. "I just wish this book had more than one chapter on buried treasure."

"Let's look online," Bryan said.

They huddled around one of the library computers and searched for the wildest stories they could find. Bryan scrolled down a webpage, passing an outlined landscape that looked familiar to Julian.

"Wait—go back!" Julian pointed to the screen. The map didn't have any of the roads or buildings that were there today, but he'd recognize Silver Lake anywhere. "That's not far from here."

The boys read the story of a stagecoach full of gold that had been held up by bandits. Bryan read a little faster than Julian, but he waited patiently as Julian scrolled down the page at his own pace. The bandits were afraid of getting caught, so they had buried the stolen gold near the lake. But they never came back for it. As far as anyone knew, half a million dollars' worth of gold was still out there somewhere. And it was so close to where they lived!

"Can you imagine finding it?" Bryan asked.

Julian shook his head. "I can't believe that lake isn't swarmed with people looking for this treasure."

"I practically spent the whole summer at that lake," Bryan said. "We'd just moved here, and I had nothing else to do. What if there was gold right there that whole time?"

Julian wished he'd known Bryan over the summer. They could've hung out after reading camp, exploring the lake and searching yard sales for maps and other treasures. He wondered if Bryan had ever seen the Winderhouser place. He thought Bryan would be as fascinated by Mrs. Winderhouser's collection as he was. Plus, he'd get to see where Star came from.

But Julian didn't get a chance to ask. Someone cleared his throat loudly behind the boys, making them jump.

"Julian, Bryan—you've already finished your assignment?" Their teacher's voice was full of doubt. Everyone knew that reading assignments took Julian forever.

Julian's face warmed, and he cast a glance toward Bryan. Even though Bryan knew about his dyslexia, Julian didn't want him to know how poorly he was doing in school.

"I . . . I thought I could finish it at home," Julian stammered. There was no way he could do it on his own before class was over.

"Sorry, Mr. Helmer," Bryan said quickly. "I asked Julian to show me something."

Mr. Helmer made a big show of checking his watch. "There's still fifteen minutes left in the period. You might be able to finish it."

Julian waited until Mr. Helmer walked away. Then he took one final glance at the Silver Lake map before pushing back his chair. "I better get back to it."

Bryan closed the window and logged out of the computer. "I haven't finished mine either. We can do it together."

Julian's spirits lifted a little. He hated getting into trouble, and if the two of them could work together, maybe they would get it done more quickly. He was starting to think they could do anything, even find buried treasure that had stayed hidden for hundreds of years. After all, they'd cracked the code on how to communicate with Star. Julian wrapped his fingers around the dog tag and smiled at his friend.

# ★ CHAPTER 10 ★

**Julian and Bryan** huddled outside Ms. Khan's office on Saturday morning. They'd spent the whole lunch period on Friday planning this out. They'd made a lot of progress with Star, but she couldn't stay in the socialization room forever. It was time to take her outside so she could sniff the trees and grass and run around like a normal dog.

Ms. Khan opened the door, and Julian was greeted by a chunky tan pit bull mix. The dog's tail wagged in circles like a helicopter blade, and his tongue hung out of his mouth in a giant smile.

"Hey, Buster!" Bryan said, patting the dog's big,

square head. Of course he knew the animal by name, Julian thought.

"I need to do some work with Buster today." Ms. Khan snapped a leash on the mutt's collar. His tail spun even faster. "I'm hoping if I wear him out a bit, he'll stop trying to eat his blankets."

Julian's heart sank. "Does that mean we can't work with Star?"

"Of course you can! She really needs you." Ms. Khan took another leash off a hook and held it out. "How do you feel about getting her out of the kennel yourself?"

"Sure!" Julian felt like his heart actually skipped a beat. He cleared his throat, trying not to appear as excited as he felt. "I mean, I think I can do that." He took the black nylon leash from Ms. Khan.

"Definitely," Bryan said, turning to Ms. Khan. "Can we take her to the training yard today?"

"That's a great idea." Ms. Khan handed Star's vibration collar and remote to Bryan. "I'll be walking Buster, so I can stay close in case you have any problems."

Armed with the leash, treats, and his determination to get this right, Julian marched up to Star's kennel. She watched him approach, her ears tipped forward and her tail swaying uncertainly. The black Lab mix in the kennel next to hers saw the leash and started barking and hopping on his front feet. That set off a barking chain up and down the kennels, and soon it was impossibly loud. Julian looked at Star, hoping she wasn't scared. But, of course, the noise didn't bother her.

"Here goes." Julian took a deep breath, opened the door of her kennel, and stepped inside. He gave her a thumbs-up and a treat. She leaned against his leg, and he stroked the gray patches on her back.

"I can't believe you're in there with her," Bryan said as he closed the kennel door behind Julian. "I mean, she's been doing so well, but I never thought I'd see this!"

"Now the trick is getting her *out* of here." Julian exhaled slowly and snapped the leash on Star's purple collar. He quickly clasped the vibration collar around her neck and gave her another treat. She didn't even flinch. As she looked up at him with her bright, curious eyes, Julian let out a relieved sigh. Now he had to get her outside.

"Just lure her along with treats," Bryan said. "As long as the leash isn't pulling on her, I think she'll be okay."

Julian nodded. They'd gone over leash training a dozen times yesterday at lunch, and he'd spent lots of time walking Star in circles around the socialization room to get her used to being on the lead. He knew exactly what he was supposed to do. He just didn't know if Star would freak out once she got out of her kennel.

He took a backward step toward the door and held out a treat. Star didn't move.

Julian glanced over his shoulder at Bryan with a look of worry. He didn't want to pull on the leash, but if Star didn't move on her own, they were going to be out of luck.

He turned back toward her, the leash still slack

between them, and knelt down. He gave Star the hand signal for *come* that his grandpa had taught him. "It's okay, girl. I know it's scary."

Star hesitated for a second, then timidly trotted forward. She gently took the treat from Julian's outstretched palm. He did it two more times, and they made it to the kennel door.

Bryan slowly opened the door. Star's gaze whipped from Julian to the doorway, her eyes going wide. Julian stepped into the aisle. Star stayed frozen in her kennel. Julian held out a treat, and Star cautiously inched forward until she reached him. He gave her a thumbs-up and petted her, hoping to reassure her. She trembled beside him. "You'll love it outside, Star," he said softly. "There's grass and dirt and fresh air. You can't stay in here forever."

She may not have been able to hear him, but she calmed down a little. Julian stepped backwards like he had in the kennel and gave her a treat when she came along with him. It was hard to stay focused on her with the other dogs barking and jumping around in their kennels. Even Star got distracted. She walked in a low crouch and sneaked glances at the other dogs between treats.

They inched down the kennel aisle two steps at a time. Bryan stayed ten feet behind them, so Star wouldn't feel crowded. Julian had never walked this slowly in his life. He glanced up. The door was only twenty-five feet away and then they'd be outside. They could do this.

Julian took another step, but Star must've been distracted, because the leash was now stretched between them.

Star started to panic.

She made that horrible screaming sound and jerked back and forth the way she had on the first day. Her body was writhing in circular movements, like a corkscrew, and the sounds of her high-pitched shrieks echoed through the air. It was like she was shaking off all the progress they'd made.

Bryan stood behind Star like a statue, his eyes as wide as hers. Julian wondered if Bryan was afraid that getting involved would only make Star more scared. Or maybe Bryan was just as freaked out as he was.

Julian didn't know what to do. Now that they weren't in the socialization room or her kennel, he couldn't drop her leash the way he had the last time. He reached into his pocket for the remote to her vibration collar and realized that it was still in Bryan's hand.

Julian dropped to his knees and waved his free hand to get her attention. Star stopped flailing around and looked at him, as if she were surprised to find him there. She ran up to him, nearly bowling him over, and leaned against his side for comfort. Julian stroked her fur as she trembled, and they sat like that for a moment, together.

He got to his feet and took a tentative step toward the door, bracing himself for Star to panic again. But she stayed by his side. She looked up at him, her eyes full of trust, pleading to get her out of there. So he did.

Julian started walking, then quickly picked up speed. Star kept pace with him, and soon he was racing to the door, the dog running alongside him. They burst outside into the sunshine and kept running until they'd reached the shade beneath a huge tree. Bryan joined them, and the three of them breathed in the fresh air. Star's tongue hung out of her mouth, and her nose twitched as she looked around for the first time. The sun painted shadows of branches over the grass. It had rained that morning, and the ground was soft and damp. The air smelled like wet leaves.

Julian saw Ms. Khan working with Buster on the walking path. She glanced up at them, and he waved to let her know everything was okay. But Julian wasn't a hundred percent sure that it was. Even though the leash dangled loosely between them, he could see the tension in Star's muscles as she took everything in.

"Let's take her to the yard," Bryan suggested. "It's fenced in, so she can run around."

Julian wasn't sure that either of them was ready to move from the spot under the tree, but he liked the idea of giving Star more freedom. Maybe she wouldn't be so scared if she didn't have to worry about the leash tugging on her collar while she got used to the sights and scents of the outdoors.

Bryan led the way to the yard. Star stayed close to Julian, her eyes darting all around. Once the gates were safely latched behind them, Julian dropped the leash so she could run and play. But she didn't do either of those things. She stuck like glue to Julian's side, her eyes as big as golf balls and her nostrils flaring in and out. Her muscles twitched as she looked one way, then the other, and she hid behind Julian's legs as if she were facing invisible monsters.

Julian waggled his fingers at her, but she ignored him. He looked at Bryan nervously. "What's up with her?" He knew that Star couldn't hear the dogs barking or other sounds from inside the shelter. There wasn't much activity on this stretch of road. With leaves drifting from the trees in the autumn sunshine, the yard seemed peaceful to Julian. But Star's tail stayed tucked between her legs.

Bryan shook his head and furrowed his brow. "She's probably just jumpy from being outside for the first time. Try giving her a command. It might help her calm down."

Julian tried waving at Star again, but she wouldn't look at him. He took the remote from Bryan and gave her collar a quick buzz. She did a little jump-spin to face him, but she kept her head lowered, like she was in trouble.

"It's okay, girl. It's just me." Julian squatted down to her level and stretched out his hand. She gave his knuckles a tentative lick but kept her tail tucked. Julian held out a treat. His palms were so sweaty he thought he might drop it on the ground. Star's anxiety was making him nervous. She sniffed the treat but didn't take it, almost as if she'd forgotten all the training and trust they'd built up.

"She's really scared," Julian said. "I think this is too much for her."

"She needs time to get used to it," Bryan said. "Too bad my mom didn't make chicken last night."

Julian was pretty sure that all the chicken in the world wouldn't be enough to make Star feel better about being outdoors. She just wasn't ready.

"We should take her back inside." He stood up slowly, wiping his palms on his jeans, picked up the leash, and headed for the gate. Star stayed close to his legs, and he had to be careful not to trip over her. He wished he could be happy that she wanted to be near him and wasn't freaking out about the leash anymore, but he hated seeing her so terrified.

Julian walked quickly back into the shelter while Bryan went to tell Ms. Khan how it went. When they reached the kennels, Star bolted into her cage, practically dragging Julian with her.

He closed her kennel door behind them and sat on the floor, his heart racing. Star backed into a corner of the kennel, as far away from him as she could get. It seemed that they'd gone in reverse, all the way back to the first day they'd met. At least she wasn't shaking anymore.

Julian pulled his knees up to his chest and laid his forehead on his arms. He felt terrible for letting Star get so scared. He just wanted to protect her and help her feel safe, but he'd only made things worse. But just then, as a wave of doubt washed over him, he felt something cold and wet nudging his elbow. He looked up to find her beside him, pressing her nose to his arm. She looked worried about *him*. Julian smiled down at the sweet dog by his side.

"We're okay," he said, straightening his legs and unfolding his arms. He rubbed her silky ears. She tilted her head into his hand. He unclipped the leash from her collar and set it by the door. Star yawned and lay down next to him, her front legs stretched alongside his. They sat together for a long time.

# ★ CHAPTER 11 ★

**When their volunteer shift** was over, Julian and Bryan rode their bikes back to Julian's house, where a mountain of homework waited for them. It was Bryan's idea that they study together. Even though working together in social studies had gone well, getting through this amount of work was going to be tough. Julian was nervous.

They had the house to themselves. Julian's dad was at work, his mom was at Grandpa's house, and Henry was out with his friends. Julian was glad that no one would be looking over their shoulders while they muddled through their homework. He had a hard enough time doing it on his own, and he wasn't sure how it would work with a study partner.

Julian wasn't in a big hurry to hit the books. He took his time grabbing cheese sticks and a box of crackers. He brought the snack out to the dining room table, where Bryan was pulling textbooks and notebooks out of his backpack.

"I like to start with English," Bryan said. "That way I can get the hard stuff out of the way and save math for last."

"Sure." Julian tried to sound like it didn't matter either way. But he was the opposite. He usually started with the easier subjects to put off reading as long as he could. Sometimes he put it off forever, which was what kept landing him in detention.

His stomach knotted with worry as he took out the novel they were reading that unit. They were supposed to read two chapters over the weekend and answer a bunch of questions. Even though he knew Bryan had dyslexia, too, he was still nervous. What if Bryan thought Julian was slowing him down?

What if he ended up judging him, just like everyone else did?

Julian had only done homework with his parents, so he wasn't sure where to start with Bryan. "Should we read it out loud? Or read a couple pages to ourselves and check in? I'm really slow."

"I'm no speed reader either." Bryan took out his phone and set it on the table. "But I've got the audiobook. We can listen together."

"You mean listen to other people read the book?" Julian asked. Was Bryan doing that when he had his headphones on in the cafeteria?

"It's really cool." Bryan's eyes lit up. "They do voices and everything. And listening makes it easier for me to follow the text and understand the story. It's helped my reading a lot. I think you'll like it."

Julian was doubtful that he'd like anything that had to do with reading, but he was willing to give it a try.

"Okay, let's do it." Julian opened his book and got out a ruler.

Bryan paused, his finger hovering over his phone. "What's that for?"

"It's something I learned at st—" Julian stopped himself from saying *stupid kids' camp*. He and Bryan weren't dumb; they just learned differently. He needed to start thinking of these tools as . . . signals. They were *reading* signals, just like Star's hand signals. "It's a trick from reading camp. The ruler makes it easier to focus on just one line at a time."

"Can I try?" Bryan asked. Julian gave him his silver ruler and found an old blue plastic one in the kitchen junk drawer for himself. When Julian sat back down at the table, Bryan looked at him. "Ready?"

Julian nodded. They lined up their rulers at the start of the chapter. Bryan hit play.

For once, Julian got into the story. Between the audiobook and the ruler, he was able to follow along. As he listened to the reader do different voices, he felt like he understood the characters. It still took all his concentration to keep up, but hearing the words made it easier. It also helped to know that Bryan was following along at the same pace. Before Julian knew it, the first chapter was over.

Bryan hit pause. "Need a break?"

Julian rubbed his eyes. "I can't believe we already read the whole chapter. I kind of want to know what happens next."

"Me too." Bryan grinned and hit play. By the time they got to the end of their assigned reading, Julian knew that he had to download the audiobook. The main character had just started his training to take over the most important role in his society. The more he learned, the more the character realized that he was seeing the world differently than his friends and family saw it, and that was going to change everything. Julian could relate. He even wanted to listen to the earlier chapters of the book that he'd skipped or struggled through with his parents.

Julian and Bryan helped each other answer the questions about the chapters. When they finished, Julian felt lighter. They still had science and math homework, but his worst subject hadn't been so bad for once—and it was done.

Bryan slid his science textbook from the pile of books. "Sorry, no audiobook for this one."

"I've got something that might help." Julian ran to his room and got his laptop. He typed the chapter topic into the search engine. "There are usually vlogs and other videos about everything we're learning in science. Some of them are really funny. I usually watch a couple, so at least I know a little bit before trying to read the chapter."

"I never thought of that," Bryan said. "That's really smart."

Julian flushed with pride as he pulled up a video. The best student in his grade had just called him smart!

By the time they got to their math homework, the cheese and crackers were gone and Julian and Bryan were joking around. Julian heard the garage door rumble, and a minute later his dad came through the door.

Julian's dad sat down at the head of the table in his scrubs. He'd been on a double shift at the hospital, and he looked like he needed to crawl into bed. "You must be Bryan," he said.

Bryan nodded. "That's me."

"It's nice to finally meet you." Julian's dad surveyed the cheese wrappers, the books scattered all over the table, the laptop, Bryan's phone, and the boys' smiles. "But Julian needs to get his homework done. Do you need a ride home?"

"Dad!" Julian protested. "Can't he stay for dinner?"

"Jules, we've talked about this." His dad looked at Bryan. "Sorry, but—"

"—my homework is done!" Julian interrupted.

"All of it?" His dad sounded skeptical.

"We just finished up math," Bryan said.

"Great. And . . . what about your reading?" Julian's dad asked carefully.

Julian waved the work sheet with the completed questions. "We did that first."

His dad's tired eyes widened in surprise as he looked over the work sheet. "Wow! I'm really proud of you, Julian. Okay, as long as it's okay with your parents, Bryan, you're welcome to stay."

Julian's heart swelled with pride. It had been a long time since he'd impressed his parents with schoolwork.

Bryan called his mom to get permission to stay for

dinner while Julian packed up his books. Then they tromped upstairs to Julian's room. Bryan went right to the bookshelf that teemed with Julian's map collection. "Whoa—you weren't kidding. This is amazing!"

He picked up an old map of the Upper Peninsula and carefully unfolded it. As Bryan studied the map on the floor, Julian opened his sketchbook.

"Do you know about Mrs. Winderhouser?" Julian asked.

Bryan looked up. "You mean the old lady who owned Star? Not really. Except I heard Ms. Khan say once that she was a hoarder."

"Her house is in my neighborhood," Julian said. "A lot of people complain about all the junk around her house, but I don't see it that way."

He flipped his sketchbook open to the map he was working on of the old house, and he passed it to Bryan. He'd never shown it to anyone, and he nibbled the edge of his fingernail as Bryan looked closely at the drawing, just as he had at the antique map.

"There's so much here." Bryan's voice was filled with wonder. "Talk about buried treasure."

"Exactly!" Julian lowered himself to the floor beside Bryan so they could study the sketch together. "I like to think about where all her stuff came from and what's in the house that we don't even know about. I mean, no one knew about Star."

"What's going to happen to all of it?" Bryan asked.

Julian shrugged. "I don't know. I heard my parents say that someone needs to clean it all out. But I guess they have to find out if she has any relatives or a will or something before anyone can go in there."

"I hope you finish your map first," Bryan said.

"I'm going to try," Julian said. It was a big project. But with his new homework techniques, maybe he'd have more time in the evenings to work on it.

# ★ CHAPTER 12 ★

**The next day,** Julian and Bryan got Ms. Khan's permission to try taking Star outside again. This time the dog was waiting by the kennel door. When she spotted Julian, her tail swished back and forth in a single wag. It was so quick, Julian almost missed it. But he didn't, and that one little wag gave him the confidence he needed.

He stepped into her kennel. "Ready to try again, Star? Wanna go outside?"

She couldn't hear him, but she could sense that he was excited. She wove around his legs and lifted her head, as if letting him know she was ready for the leash. He snapped it onto her collar and gave her a treat. He put on her vibration collar and checked to make sure the remote was in his pocket. Bryan opened the door for them and stood back.

Star didn't exactly race out of the kennel. She crept to the door and poked her head around the corner. The black Lab mix had been adopted that morning, so the kennel next to Star's was empty. That seemed to help her relax enough to scuttle out of her enclosure and jog alongside Julian the rest of the way to the outside door. This was already going much better than last time.

Eager to build on their progress, Julian took her straight to the yard. Bryan ran behind them to catch up and close the gate. Julian dropped Star's leash and waited to see what she'd do. Through the chainlink fence, he could see Ms. Khan teaching Buster commands on the far end of the walking path. Julian knew that she was keeping an eye on them. He hoped he wouldn't have to bring Star in so soon today.

Star's nose twitched like crazy as a breeze blew through the yard, but she didn't seem as freaked out as she had been the day before. The look in her eyes seemed more worried than terrified. And she shifted her weight on her paws instead of standing stiff like a statue. She dipped her head to sniff the grass, then looked up at Julian. He gave her a thumbs-up and a treat, hope filling his chest as she took it. But then she dropped it into the grass.

"So close," Bryan said. "She's doing so much better today . . . wait! Look—she picked up the treat!"

Sure enough, Star had decided to eat the treat after all. Julian took that as a good sign.

He reached down to pet her, but all of a sudden she whipped her head around to stare at the ribbon of street visible through the fence. Startled by her movement, the boys followed her gaze. In the distance, sunlight glinted off a car. Star watched it until her attention was pulled in the other direction, toward a pair of squirrels chasing each other up a tree trunk on the opposite side of the yard. The boys could barely keep up with what she was seeing, but Star didn't miss anything that was happening around them. This time she wasn't paralyzed with fear—this was a different kind of stress, almost as if someone had cranked up her senses and her head was spinning with all the new sights and smells.

"Dogs have a sense of smell that's a hundred thousand times greater than ours," Bryan said, his eyes as wide as Star's as he watched her take in the world around her. "She's sniffing stuff we can't even imagine. And I bet her nose is even stronger because she can't hear."

"What if she's more sensitive to *everything* because she can't hear?" Julian's chest tightened as he watched Star taking in every detail, from a light flickering in the distance to a leaf floating to the ground from the big tree in the corner of the yard. She even seemed to sense vibrations through her whiskers and paws. He knew what it felt like to be overwhelmed by so much new information. He thought about how the first day of school every year felt like a tidal wave of new subjects, teachers, textbooks, and words crashing over him. And that was just with his boring human senses. No wonder it had been too much for Star yesterday.

"She's like a superhero dog!" Bryan's voice was

filled with wonder. "It's like she just discovered her superpowers and has to learn how to control them. We're lucky she's not causing electrical storms or moving things with her mind."

Julian had never thought that seeing the world differently could be a superpower. He pictured Star flying around the yard, her tail waving behind her. Maybe, he thought, he could use some of his own tricks to help her. Whenever he got overwhelmed, he tried to focus on one thing and push everything else to the background. He reached for the remote in his pocket and gave her vibration collar a buzz.

Star turned her wide-eyed attention to him. He gave her a thumbs-up to tell her it was okay. He gave her a treat and a pat. She started to turn her head toward the squirrels and cars again, but he waved and waggled his fingers—the sign he and Grandpa had decided was her name—and she kept her eyes on him. He went through all the commands she knew. Star's body started to relax, and her expression became less frantic. The familiar commands seemed to help her calm down.

"Let's get her to run around a bit," Bryan said. "We can play tag!"

Julian scrunched his brow. "How do you play tag with a dog?"

"Easy. We take turns trying to get her to chase us, and she can tag our hands with her nose. I'll go first." Bryan took off, running to the other side of the yard, his hair bouncing. He zigzagged like a football player dodging a tackle. Star watched his every move as if she wasn't sure what to think. But when Bryan turned around and waved at her, she raced after him, bounding through the grass. He held out his hand, palm forward. When she touched her nose to it to sniff it, he gave her a treat.

"Your turn," Bryan said.

Julian started a slow jog along the fence. He glanced over his shoulder. Star stayed by Bryan's side, sniffing the grass.

"You have to act a little crazier," Bryan called across the yard. "You want her to wonder what the heck you're doing."

Julian hopped from foot to foot like an Olympic

speed skater. Star cocked her head at him. He waved his arms like they were octopus tentacles. Star crouched like a sprinter at the starting line. Julian waved, and she bounded toward him, her tongue flapping happily.

When her cold nose touched his hand, he laughed and gave her a treat. Playing tag with a dog was like a lot of Bryan's ideas—it made Julian feel a little self-conscious, but he had to admit it was fun. And it worked. Star was no longer overwhelmed by all the sights and smells around them. She trusted Julian and Bryan enough to play, probably for the first time in her life.

The boys ran around with Star until they were all panting and smiling. Julian could have stayed out there with her forever, but then something caught Star's eye on the road. Julian followed her gaze and recognized the car pulling up to the shelter. "Oh no! I forgot my parents were coming to pick me up."

Bryan checked the big black watch he always wore around his wrist. "I can't believe how long we've been out here. I guess we better get Star back in her kennel."

Star didn't even flinch when Julian snapped the leash onto her collar. He opened the gate and gave her the *watch me* signal he'd learned online. He figured that if she kept her eyes on him, she'd stay close enough to keep the leash from pulling on her collar as they walked back to the shelter. But he was so focused on keeping Star's attention that he almost ran right into Ms. Khan and Buster.

Ms. Khan quickly shortened the slack in Buster's leash and pulled him in close to her side. "Hey! I was just coming to check on you guys."

Buster strained against the leash, his mouth open in a big grin and his nose stretching toward Star. His tail whirled around and around.

Julian's heart caught in his throat. He hadn't been expecting Ms. Khan to be right on the other side of the gate. He worried that the other dog might scare Star. She probably hadn't met another dog nose to nose since she was a puppy, before she lived with Mrs. Winderhouser. But Star took a shy step toward Buster, her tail swishing in a tentative wag. Ms. Khan came closer and let the two dogs greet each other. They sniffed at each other's ears and tails. The pit bull gently licked Star's ear. Julian wondered if he sensed something different about her.

"I don't think she's ever been around other dogs." Ms. Khan spoke softly, as if she didn't want to interrupt the dogs. "This is a really big deal!"

"This is like her tenth big deal of the day," Bryan said.

Ms. Khan laughed. "So—she did well in the training yard?"

"She was awesome," Julian said. "She ran around and everything."

"I can't believe how much progress you've made with her," Ms. Khan said.

"It was mostly Julian." Bryan smiled. "She really loves him."

Julian dug the toe of his sneaker into the dirt. "All the stuff you know about dogs really helped," he said to Bryan.

Ms. Khan looked between the two of them. "Whatever the secret is, you two have made such a difference."

Julian heard the sound of his parents' car doors in the parking lot. "I better get her back inside."

"We'll all go in." Ms. Khan led Buster toward the shelter ahead of them. He kept tugging and looking back toward Star until he was halfway to the door. Then he finally paid attention to the treat Ms. Khan offered him and followed her inside. Julian waited until the door closed behind them. He used his hand signals to get Star walking beside him again. She trotted calmly all the way inside and through the kennels, ignoring the other dogs as she passed them. As soon as they were in her kennel, Julian unclipped the leash and removed the vibration collar. She took a big drink of water, then curled up on her blanket, exhilarated and exhausted from her big day.

Julian was still smiling when he met his parents in the lobby. Ms. Khan had put Buster in his kennel, and she came up to say hello. "Julian is doing an amazing job," she said. "Your son has a real gift with animals."

His dad raised his eyebrows. "Really?"

Ms. Khan nodded. "You should come meet the dog he's been working with."

Julian could've hugged her right then and there. He'd been trying to think of a way to get his parents to meet Star, and it seemed to him that Ms. Khan had read his mind. But even though this was exactly what he wanted, his stomach did slow somersaults as his parents followed Ms. Khan down the hallway toward the kennels. Star wasn't outgoing like most of the other dogs in the shelter. What if she acted afraid—like she had on the first day? What if his parents didn't like her at all?

His heart started to thump nervously. When they gathered outside her kennel, Star lifted her head sleepily from her paws to look at what was probably the largest group of people she'd ever seen. Julian wanted to drag his parents away. This many people crowded around her could send her cowering into the corner. But when Star spotted Julian, she stood up and stretched, unfurling her tongue in a giant yawn. She shook out her fur from head to tail, as if shaking off sleep, then walked right up to where Julian squatted on the other side of the cage. She leaned against the metal wire, letting him scratch her head. Then she looked up at his parents with her bashful blue eyes.

She was acting like the dog Julian had sensed was inside of her the moment he first met her.

"She's so sweet." His mom's voice had the sappy tone it got whenever she was around the neighbor's baby.

"She is!" Julian said.

"She seems like a really good dog," Julian's dad said.

Ms. Khan winked at Julian. "You wouldn't believe what Star was like when she first got here. Julian is the one who turned her around. He's been working really hard with her."

Julian's parents looked from him to the dog and back again, their eyes wide with surprise—and maybe a little dewy with emotion from Ms. Khan's praise.

The grownups headed back toward the front of the shelter, but Julian lingered by Star's kennel. He couldn't hear what Ms. Khan was saying to his parents as they walked away, but she gestured enthusiastically. His parents glanced back at Julian and smiled, and there was something in their faces that he'd been wanting to see for so long: pride. His parents were proud of him. They were seeing for the first time that he'd found something he was really good at. What they didn't realize was that he had also found someone who needed him. He'd found Star.

Julian was grateful that Ms. Khan had let him work with Star and that his parents had let him keep volunteering. Every time he walked into the shelter, he could feel the stress of school lifting from his shoulders. He loved everything about his volunteer shifts —Star most of all. And now his parents had finally met her.

"Good girl, Star." Julian reached his fingers through the door to scratch behind her ear one more time before hurrying after his parents.

On the drive home, his mom and dad asked him all about Star and how he'd been training her. They kept saying how cute she was and how sweet she seemed. They'd met her for only a few seconds, but he could tell they'd already started to fall in love with her. Who could resist her, once they got to know her?

"We're really proud of you," his mom said. "And we've noticed that you've been better about keeping up with your homework and chores since you started volunteering at the shelter. I think training Star is helping your confidence and self-discipline."

"It is," Julian said. "I really want to help her."

"Ms. Khan says that you've made more progress with her than anyone ever expected," his dad said. "She said that lots of other people might have gotten frustrated and given up on her, but you've really stuck with it. Keep up the good work."

"I will." This was one promise Julian knew he'd have no problem keeping. He watched the trees and houses zip past the car window as they drove toward home. For the first time, he believed that if he could help Star come out of her shell, maybe he could bring her home. He closed his eyes and imagined her riding in the back seat with him as part of the family.

# ★ CHAPTER 13 ★

**Ms. Hollin strode up and down** the rows of desks, passing back homework assignments from the week before. She laid them face-down on each student's desk. Julian bounced his leg nervously as he waited for the teacher to reach his row. He had worked really hard on the assignment and felt good about the reading techniques Bryan had taught him. But what if he still got everything wrong? He glanced across the classroom at his friend. Bryan gave him a thumbs-up. Julian smiled at the encouragement. Ever since they'd started training Star, they seemed to have their own secret language.

Then Ms. Hollin got to Julian's desk. Usually she handed back his assignment and kept walking, and he just stuffed his homework in his bag without even looking at it. But today Ms. Hollin paused beside him. "Great job, Julian. I can tell you really understood the reading."

Julian could hardly believe his ears. He couldn't remember the last time a teacher had told him he did something right! He flipped over the paper and gaped at the B+ scrawled in red pen at the top of the page. It was the highest grade he'd gotten in English all year. He couldn't wait to show his parents.

"Thanks," he mumbled. He was proud of himself, but he didn't know what to do with the sudden attention.

Ms. Hollin smiled at him before moving on, and Julian couldn't stop staring at his grade.

"There's a first time for everything, huh?" Hunter mumbled from the back row. A smattering of snickers spread across the classroom behind Julian. He felt his face turning as red as the B+ on his homework. He quickly turned over the sheet, as if that could hide his shame.

"Knock it off," Bryan said loudly, and a couple of kids gasped in surprise. Bryan never spoke out of turn in class. Julian shot his friend a grateful look. He knew Bryan was no stranger to being bullied, and it was really brave of him to stand up to Hunter that way.

"No one asked you," Hunter said.

"Yeah, well, it's none of your business how other people do on their homework," Bryan said.

"Bryan Walter, no talking during class." Ms. Hollin's voice was stern. She didn't say a word to Hunter or any of the kids who had been laughing at Julian.

"But . . ." Bryan protested.

Ms. Hollin shook her head. "You know better. I don't want to have to give you detention."

Bryan raked a hand through his hair in frustration, but he kept his mouth shut. Ms. Hollin turned back to the whiteboard. At the back of the room, Hunter quietly high-fived his friends. Julian sat frozen at his desk, his hands spread over his homework as if it might fly away. He knew he should have said something in Bryan's defense, but it had all happened so quickly. He hadn't even had the chance to get over the shock of his good grade, and now his excitement about it evaporated in the air like steam.

He jammed the assignment into his backpack, crinkling the corner of the paper. Ms. Hollin had already moved on to assigning their homework. Julian sank low in his chair, feeling invisible once again.

Julian and Bryan rode their bikes side by side to the shelter after school. They raced each other down the final stretch. They couldn't wait to get to the dogs and get Star out of her kennel, so they could put the whole horrible, humiliating scene in English class behind them.

But when they got to the shelter, their day went from bad to worse.

Julian and Bryan burst through the door and found Ms. Khan sitting at her desk, her head in her hands. There was no sign of her usual contagious smile. For once, she didn't have Buster or any other animal hanging out in her office. She just stared at a letter on her desk, her shoulders hunched as if a giant weight sat on her back.

The boys exchanged a worried look. Neither of them wanted to ask what had happened. They had a feeling it wasn't something they wanted to hear, but they had to know.

"What's wrong?" Julian asked.

Ms. Khan didn't even look up at them. "We just lost our biggest funder."

"What do you mean?" Julian didn't understand how someone could just decide to stop helping the animals.

Ms. Khan sighed. She folded the letter and slipped it back into its envelope, as if she couldn't stand to look at it anymore. "We've relied on this foundation for years to keep us going. We were supposed to get another grant, but they ran out of money."

"How do they just run out of money?" Julian asked. He didn't know much about foundations or grants, but he thought the whole reason they existed was to give away money. He glanced at Bryan. He'd never seen his friend so quiet. Bryan stared at the floor, almost like he wasn't even listening.

"I don't know," Ms. Khan said. "Whatever happened, it's bad news for us and for the animals."

"I thought the city paid for the shelter." Bryan's voice was almost a whisper.

"A lot of people think that," Ms. Khan said. "But all the government money goes to the county shelter. We really needed a shelter in this town, so our dogs and cats wouldn't have to go to the other side of the county. And we needed a place that could work with some of the more challenging cases. Thanks to donations from the foundation and from people in our community, we've been able to help so many more animals find homes. But now we might not be able to stay open much longer."

Star was one of those challenging cases, Julian knew. He didn't want to think about what might have happened if she had gone to another shelter instead of this one. "What about the other people who donate? Can't we just ask them to give more?" he asked. He knew his parents gave money to charities every Christmas. He wondered if they'd ever donated here.

Ms. Khan shook her head. "People haven't been giving the way they used to. We really relied on that foundation money."

Bryan started pacing back and forth across the office. He was done being quiet. "What about other grants? What about a big fundraiser? What if we got cheaper dog food? Or maybe asked people to pay more for adoptions. Lots more." Bryan stopped moving and held his head in his hands. "There has to be another way."

"I wish there was," Ms. Khan said. "I've been crunching the numbers all day. If a miracle doesn't happen in the next couple of weeks, the animals won't have a home here anymore."

Julian felt like he had just been hit by a train. He looked over at Bryan and could see that his friend felt the same way. The shelter had become the most important place in the world to them. Julian no longer daydreamed about made-up places during school —instead, he thought about being here. He and Bryan blew through all their homework during their free period just so they would have time to go to the shelter after school. It was the one place where they felt safe being themselves. Helping the animals was the one thing they both knew they were really good at.

And because of the shelter, Julian's parents were finally starting to see how responsible he could be.

This place had changed his life.

But Julian knew it was even more important for Star and all the other animals who didn't have anywhere else to go. Thinking about all the cages empty and quiet, the building abandoned like an old factory, made Julian's stomach churn. He could tell from the way Bryan was hugging himself that his friend felt the same way.

Julian managed to find his voice. "What does that mean for Star and all the other dogs? Where will they go?"

Ms. Khan met his gaze with sad eyes. "They'll be sent to the county shelter. If there's not enough room there, some of them might have to go to shelters in other counties or other states."

The idea of Star being sent to another state felt like a punch in the gut to Julian.

"Isn't there anywhere closer?" he asked.

"Most of these shelters are overcrowded," Ms.

Khan said. "We'll have to send the animals wherever we can find room for them."

Julian looked around the lobby. The tangerine-colored walls seemed to fade into a sunset. He tried to imagine the shelters Ms. Khan was describing. In his mind, they were dark and crowded caves. He pictured staff so overworked that they always looked like Ms. Khan did now—defeated and sad instead of cheerful. A dog like Star wouldn't stand a chance in a place like that. She'd be so terrified. No one would have the time to learn her hand signals or to take it slow with her on the leash. Even if she went to the closest shelter, it was too far away for Julian to ride his bike to visit her.

"But how do we know they'll take good care of them?" Bryan asked. "Do they even have yards for the dogs to play in?"

"We don't know," Ms. Khan admitted. "They're good places and they try to find homes for as many dogs and cats as they can. But if the shelter gets over-crowded, some of the animals may have to be put down."

Julian's skin felt too tight. He shivered, as if some-one had poured ice down his back. He couldn't lose Star this way. Buster and Bumble and Pip and all the other dogs he saw every day might disappear forever — and all because there wasn't enough money or space to wait until they got adopted? He couldn't let this hap-pen. To any of them.

Julian felt like everything was falling apart around him. He looked at Bryan, knowing that his friend was thinking the same thing: they had to find a way to save Star and all the other animals. Julian just wished he knew how.

# ★ CHAPTER 14 ★

**Julian and Bryan took Star outside,** but neither of the boys felt much like playing. Star was getting braver, sniffing around the yard on her own. But she kept coming back to Julian and sitting at his feet, her paw resting on his shoe. The tips of her ears flopped back as she looked up at him with her bright blue eyes.

"I'm glad Star doesn't know what's going on," Julian said. She was just getting used to being there, and if the shelter closed, she'd lose everything she knew all over again. Worst of all, they'd lose each other. It was a crushing thought. His chest tightened, and he shoved his hands into his pockets. He couldn't even give Star the sign that things were okay.

"I think she knows something's wrong," Bryan said. "She doesn't want to leave your side."

The boys walked slowly around the yard, Star at their heels. Bryan picked up a dirty old tennis ball that was half buried beneath the leaves and looked at it sadly.

"Ms. Khan will come up with something, right?" Julian said, patting Star's head, hoping to reassure her —and himself.

"Right." Bryan tossed the old tennis ball up in the air and caught it. "We shouldn't give up hope. At least for Star's sake."

Bryan waved the ball in front of Star and threw it. When she didn't go after it right away, he did, as if challenging her to a race. Star threw a quick glance at Julian, but she couldn't resist chasing after Bryan and the ball. She beat Bryan to it, then brought the ball back to Julian.

Julian picked up the ball and threw it. Soon they were all chasing one another around the yard. It was hard not to smile as Star plowed through the piles of fallen leaves and pranced around with the ball in her mouth. By the time they put her back in her kennel, the two boys felt a little better. They'd managed to push the fate of the shelter to the back of their minds.

But the next day was one day closer to the shelter closing. Julian and Bryan tried to keep their heads up, but they couldn't stop thinking about what was going to happen to the animals.

"I can't just sit around and study for some dumb science quiz," Bryan said as they walked to Julian's house after they left the shelter. It was the first time Julian had ever heard his friend complain about homework. But Julian felt the same way. There was no way they'd be able to concentrate when their world was upside down.

"I have an idea." Julian turned onto Stagecoach Road and headed toward the Winderhouser place. The first time he'd shown Bryan the house, Bryan had been just as amazed as he was by all the stuff. They'd been back a few times since then to work on Julian's map.

When they got to the house, the boys crept across the front yard and around to the back porch. Near the back door a woven rug created a rectangle of space between the broken furniture and the stacked boxes. The boys could sit there and draw, hidden from view in case any neighbors passed by.

They sat on the dusty rug, with Julian's sketchbook between them. The map of the backyard and porch filled the page. Julian was eager to work more on mapping the inside of the house, but he hadn't quite figured out how. It was one thing to sit on the porch, but opening the door and walking around inside someone else's home felt like crossing a line. Even if the house was abandoned.

"I think this part's done." Bryan picked up the sketchbook and squinted at the section for the backyard. "I'm going to make sure we didn't miss anything." He took the sketchbook, trotted down the porch steps, and walked slowly from one end of the porch to the other, scanning the map as he went.

While Bryan checked their work, Julian dug around in his backpack for a granola bar. He thought he'd left one in there from lunch last week. His fingers brushed across the folded edges of the maps he kept on hand for when he needed something to do during lunch or his free period. But since he'd been hanging out with Bryan, he hadn't needed the maps as much. He pulled out a stack and started looking them over.

One was a map of Canada. He set that one aside. The second showed all the counties in Michigan. Julian wondered where the animal shelters were in each county. He could look it up online when he got home and mark every shelter on this map, so he'd know where Star might end up. A lump rose in his throat, and he quickly refolded the worn paper. He couldn't let them take Star away.

He slowly unfolded the last map. This one was older than the other two. His mom had found it at a used bookstore and surprised him with it. She'd said it was a reward for how well he was doing in school lately. This was a much more local map than the other two. It showed their town as it looked a hundred years ago, back in the days of logging camps and outlaws.

Something clicked in Julian's mind, and his thoughts shone like a spotlight on a big, wild idea. He shot to his feet, the map in his hand. "We need to find the treasure!"

Bryan stood at the bottom of the porch steps. He looked around the yard in confusion. "What treasure?"

"Don't you remember that story we saw online? There's half a million dollars buried out at Silver Lake." Julian gestured excitedly as the idea bubbled out of him. "It's practically right in our own backyard. If we find it, we can save the shelter!"

Bryan climbed back onto the porch, doubt written all over his face. "The one supposedly left there by bandits? But people have been looking for it for decades."

"And it's still out there!" Julian said.

"No one knows that for sure," Bryan said.

"No one knows for sure it's *not* there," Julian insisted. "That's why we have to go find it."

Bryan cocked his head the way Star did sometimes. "You're really serious?"

Julian pointed to himself. "I have all kinds of maps." He pointed at Bryan. "And you know the history. If anyone can find the treasure, it's us."

Bryan laughed. "You are the strangest kid I've ever met. Which is really a lot coming from me. But I'm in."

Julian grinned. He knew he'd be able to count on Bryan. The boys bumped their knuckles together. They were going treasure hunting.

Julian was ready to head to the lake right then, but Bryan insisted that they needed a plan. "It'll be dark soon," Bryan said, looking up at the sky. "And even darker around the lake. We don't have flashlights or shovels or anything."

Julian glanced around the porch. Mrs. Winderhouser probably had shovels and tools somewhere. But it would be much easier to follow the map in daylight. Besides, it was a huge lake and they didn't have weeks to search it.

"Let's figure out exactly where this treasure is." Julian spread out the map on the old rug.

Bryan took a notebook and pen from his own backpack. "I'll make a list of supplies. We want to be ready for anything."

"Good idea," Julian said. Now that Bryan had agreed to go along with Julian's big, crazy idea, he'd switched into serious planning mode.

Bryan leaned over the map. "How do we know where to start? It wasn't like that story gave us coordinates on where to search."

Julian played out the story in his head as if it were a movie. He could see the bandits galloping away from the stagecoach after they'd robbed it, then sneaking around the lake with their gold. "The bandits would've needed to stay close to roads to move the gold quickly, right? And they didn't want to get caught. They'd stay away from any camps where people might see them."

He ran his finger along the winding roads and old logging camps on the map. With a pencil, he circled half a dozen areas around Silver Lake that weren't too crowded or remote. He frowned at the map. "How will we dig up all these sites?" he asked.

Bryan sat up straight, as if he'd been zapped by an idea. "Maybe people posted where they've already looked."

He took out his phone and tapped at the screen, nodding to himself as he read. Then he turned Julian's map toward himself. He took the pencil and checked off the places where other people had already searched. When he was done, the boys stared at the map.

"Western Island." Bryan pointed to the only spot still circled.

"That's got to be it!" Julian's heart was racing. He felt, deep down, that this was going to work. "How will we carry it all back with us?"

"First we have to get out there and find it." Bryan began writing in his notebook. "We'll need a compass, flashlights, and extra batteries. We'll need tools to dig it up when we find it . . ."

Julian liked the way Bryan said *when we find it*, as if the treasure were already theirs. His hands tingled with excitement. He clenched them into fists, trying to focus on the plan Bryan was laying out.

"I can make sandwiches in the morning," Julian offered. "I can put all the snacks in my backpack."

"And water," Bryan said. "We should probably clean out our backpacks tonight so there's room for all the supplies."

"And the treasure." Julian was so excited he didn't

think he'd be able to sleep that night. They were really doing this! He wished he had a metal detector and a folding shovel. He wondered if Mrs. Winderhouser had treasure-hunting supplies buried somewhere in her house. He wondered what the best snacks were for finding treasure.

"We'll go to the shelter as usual tomorrow," Bryan said.

"Won't that waste too much time?" Julian asked.

"Our parents and Ms. Khan expect us to be there," Bryan said. "If we at least show up, they won't suspect anything."

Julian hadn't thought about his parents' reaction. They'd never let him go all the way out to Silver Lake on his own. He was glad that Bryan was so good at thinking through all the details.

"That makes sense," Julian said. "The shelter is on the way to Silver Lake anyway." He carefully folded the map, with the circle around Western Island facing out. He wished he had a way to tell Star that they had a plan to save her.

# ★ CHAPTER 15 ★

**Julian and Bryan arrived** at the shelter like it was any old day. Julian was secretly glad they needed to check in there first, because he didn't want to miss the chance to play with Star. He figured they would get Star outside to run around the yard, then tuck her back in her kennel and take off for Silver Lake.

But they hadn't counted on Ms. Khan saying no when they went to her office to get Star's vibration collar.

"I really need your help before you take Star out," Ms. Khan said. "Two of my staffers are out with the flu, so there's no one to help hose down cages this afternoon."

Julian and Bryan exchanged a glance. They didn't have much of a choice. Julian wished they'd thought to call in sick, too, but then he wouldn't have gotten to see Star at all. The slight delay was worth it. "Sure, we can do that," he said.

Relief washed over Ms. Khan's face. "Thank you so much. That's one less thing for me to worry about. We had to move around a bunch of the cats to deep clean the cages this morning, so the carriers that need to be cleaned are out back."

The boys nodded and left the office. Once the door was closed behind them, they raced down the hall, eager to finish the task as quickly as possible. But when they burst outside and saw the mountain of plastic cat carriers and small wire cages, they stopped in their tracks.

"This is going to take forever," Julian said. Their careful plan had been totally derailed. It felt like the treasure was getting farther away from them. "Why did they have to do the deep cleaning today?"

Bryan handed Julian the hose. "I'll open up the cages, and you start spraying."

They quickly figured out a system to clean the cages as quickly as possible, but it still took them almost an hour, and by the time they finished, the cuffs of their jeans were soaked.

When Ms. Khan finally gave them the okay to get Star, Julian hurried to the kennel. Bryan stopped him just outside the door. "Remember to act like nothing's going on. Star will know if you're anxious."

"But I *am* anxious," Julian said. "It's getting late."

"I calculated how long it'll take us to get there," Bryan said. "We still have plenty of time before dark."

Julian tried to relax. He exhaled slowly and shook out his arms. It helped that Star was so happy to see him. She pressed her cold nose into his hand and leaned against his leg. He clipped the leash to her collar, and they jogged out to the yard.

Bryan found a tennis ball, and he and Julian took turns throwing it for Star. Julian wanted to talk about their plans for finding the treasure, but Ms. Khan kept checking in on them. So he stayed quiet and focused all his attention on Star. At least it was sunny enough that their shoes and jeans began to dry. When the dog became less interested in chasing the ball and more interested in sniffing at the grass, Bryan nodded at Julian.

Julian snapped the leash onto Star's collar and waved at Ms. Khan, who was working with a young beagle. "We're taking her back in now."

"Okay," Ms. Khan said. "Thanks for letting me know!"

The boys put Star back in her kennel with lots of scratches behind the ears and a handful of treats on her bed. Julian felt guilty for not sitting with her the way he usually did, but they had to get going. He stepped out of her kennel and closed the door behind him. Star abandoned the treats on her bed and came to the kennel door. She looked up at Julian and Bryan with sad eyes.

"We better go," Bryan said.

Julian reached through the kennel door to scratch Star beneath the chin. He wished he had a sign to tell her he was sorry.

Julian and Bryan wheeled their bikes away from the shelter. Their backpacks were heavy with snacks, water bottles, maps, flashlights, and garden tools to help them dig up the treasure. They had everything they might need, but Julian still felt that something was missing. At the edge of the parking lot, Bryan swung his leg over his bike. Julian hesitated. He reached into his pocket and touched Star's tag, the way he always did when he needed reassurance.

Bryan was ready to go. "What's wrong?"

Julian ran his thumb over the engraved numbers on the tag, remembering Star's sad eyes. He felt guilty about leaving her, even though he was trying to save her. "I wish Star could come with us."

"She'd be a good treasure hunter," Bryan said. "Because she's deaf, her other senses are enhanced— like her brain kind of rewired itself to make her vision and sense of smell even better."

"What if she could sniff it out as soon as we got to Western Island?" Other treasure hunters might have metal detectors, but Star would be even better. Julian imagined her leading them right to the spot where an old treasure chest was buried. "And she'd probably be able to help us find our way back better than any compass."

Bryan didn't answer right away. He stared down the street, his eyes narrowed and one hand tugging at his hair. Finally he turned to Julian and nodded seriously. "Okay, let's do it."

"Do what?" Julian asked.

"Let's go get Star," Bryan said.

"Are you serious?" Julian tried not to get his hopes up.

"If we bring her with us, she might be able to help. Just like you said."

Julian shook his head. "Ms. Khan will never let us take her."

Bryan lowered his voice. "Ms. Khan doesn't need to know. All the dogs have been walked by now, so Ms. Khan won't be paying close attention to the kennels until dinnertime. If we're quick, no one will even notice that Star is gone."

Julian thought it over. They were breaking the rules and could get in big trouble, but this was important. How could Ms. Khan be mad when they returned with enough gold to save the shelter? He imagined the three of them coming back just as night was falling and Ms. Khan was about to start feeding the dogs. He and Bryan would be tired, slowed down by their backpacks loaded with treasure. Star would be trotting ahead of them, head high and tail wagging, knowing that she'd helped save the day. They'd sneak her back into her kennel and then surprise Ms. Khan with the gold.

Julian was convinced. It suddenly seemed that there was no way they could do this without Star.

He turned back toward the shelter. "Let's go get her."

"Wait." Bryan grabbed Julian's handlebars. "We need a plan."

Julian and Bryan hid their bikes behind some bushes at the edge of the shelter property. They wouldn't be able to ride them anyway once Star was with them, but Western Island was only five miles away, so they figured they could walk there. It would take a little longer than going on their bikes, but it was worth it to have Star with them. And Julian had packed more than enough snacks to keep them fueled for the hike.

The boys crouched behind a tree and watched the

shelter door. Ms. Khan had finished her training session with the beagle, and Bryan was pretty sure she was back in her office.

"She always goes back to her office after working with a dog—to catch up on email and stuff," Bryan whispered. "She's probably working on the budget or trying to find new grants."

"Not for long," Julian said, picturing Ms. Khan sitting in her office, stacking towering piles of gold coins.

Bryan nodded. "Okay, you go get Star. I'll keep watch."

Julian crept around the building to the back door by the kennels. He took a leash off the hook inside the door and tiptoed to Star's cage. It didn't matter how quiet he tried to be. The other dogs came to their doors as he passed. Some of them started barking. Julian shushed them, hoping Ms. Khan couldn't hear the dogs sounding the alarm all the way in her office. He gave up trying to be sneaky and raced to Star's kennel.

She was waiting by her kennel door, tail wagging, as if she'd known all along that he was coming back for her. She let him clip the leash onto her collar and practically pulled him out the door. They were halfway out of her cage when he grabbed her water bowl, sloshing the last few drops onto the kennel floor. It hadn't been on Bryan's list, but Julian thought she might get thirsty. He wondered if he should bunch up her blanket so it looked like she was asleep in the corner of her kennel. But he decided there wasn't enough time. Besides, it wouldn't fool Ms. Khan. He just had to hope she didn't come looking for Star before they got back.

Julian closed the kennel door behind him so it wouldn't draw any attention. Then he and Star ran out of the building to where Bryan waited for them. Bryan took the bowl from Julian and zipped it into his backpack. "Good thinking! She's going to need that."

Julian thought about his parents. He knew they would be upset that he was taking the dog out without permission, but he decided to push that thought to the side. He just had to trust that they'd understand once he, Star, and Bryan saved the shelter.

When Julian and Bryan turned toward the road instead of the training yard, Star stopped in her tracks.

She looked toward the yard in confusion. Julian worried that she might panic and he'd have to leave her behind after all. He wished she was wearing her vibration collar so he could get her attention, but there had been no way for him to swipe it from the office where Ms. Khan was working.

He lowered himself into a squat and waved at Star. She glanced at the yard one more time before trotting up to him. He scratched her behind the ears, then petted her patches of gray fur. "We're going on an adventure, and we need you, Star. It's okay, you're going to love it."

Star wagged her tail uncertainly. Julian gave her a reassuring thumbs-up. She tipped her head back and gently licked his chin. He stood and faced Bryan. "I think that means she's ready to go."

The boys hoisted their backpacks onto their shoulders and crossed the road. They walked quickly away from the shelter, in the opposite direction of town. As they rounded a curve in the road and the shelter disappeared behind them, Bryan let out a long exhale.

Julian felt the same sense of relief. They had made it out without being caught! They were really on their way.

The boys settled in for the long walk ahead of them. Star's nostrils flared and her whiskers twitched as she took in all the new smells and sights. She was weaving from side to side, her nose working furiously as she investigated every patch of dirt and blade of grass.

"I was a little worried that she'd be overwhelmed," Bryan confessed, swishing a stick through the tall grass beside the road. "But all that time in the training yard really paid off!"

Julian smiled, watching Star sniff a million things he couldn't even begin to imagine. She probably knew what bugs were hiding in the grass and whether any other dogs had been through there earlier and how many cars had driven down the road today. Her tail wagged as she trotted alongside them. He couldn't wait for her to see Silver Lake.

# ★ CHAPTER 16 ★

**Julian, Star, and Bryan** stopped in front of the wooden split-rail fence that blocked their path. It stretched as far as they could see in both directions. Beyond the big NO TRESPASSING sign and the remains of harvested cornstalks, they could make out a patch of woods in the distance. The land bridge to Western Island was just past those trees.

Star ducked her head beneath the bottom rail of the fence, her front paw crossing the line onto the forbidden property. Julian tapped her hip and signaled for her to come back to him. He kept an eye on the sign looming over them, as if it might come to life and yell at them for standing there.

"We need to keep moving if we're going to get Star back before dark," Bryan said, looking at the sign, then up and down the fence line blocking their path. "Is there another way?"

Julian took the map out of his backpack. The private farm hadn't existed when this old map was created, so he hadn't expected it to be there, and he had no idea how big it was. The only thing he knew for sure was that the most direct route to the treasure was across these fields.

Julian refolded the map. "We have to get to those trees."

"But it's private property," Bryan protested.

"It'll take at least three times as long if we try to go around the farm." Julian handed Star's leash to Bryan, then climbed onto the fence. He shielded his eyes and looked in both directions. "I don't see any farmhouses or tractors. There's no one around to see us."

Bryan squatted down to examine the cornstalks. "The field has already been harvested, so they probably don't have a reason to come back right now." He glanced at Star, as if asking for her opinion. She stared back at him with an expectant, *what are you waiting for?* look in her eye. Bryan stood and nodded at Julian. "Okay, let's do it."

The boys carefully climbed over the fence. They paused on the other side, as if waiting for an alarm to go off. When nothing happened, they started across the field, the brown, flattened stalks crunching beneath their shoes. Star sniffed at an ear of corn that had been left behind.

Julian and Bryan kept looking nervously over their shoulders as they trekked across the open area. The fence got smaller and smaller behind them as the trees up ahead grew taller, until soon the woods were looming just a hundred feet away. They peered anxiously at the shadows between the trunks. Star picked up on their uneasiness and stayed close to Julian. He felt reassured every time her fur brushed against his leg.

The woods had seemed so far away from the other side of the fence, but they'd made it across the field quickly—without seeing an angry landowner. Julian and Bryan started to relax, feeling confident that they'd get to the cover of the trees before anyone saw them trespassing. Bryan bent down and picked up an ear of corn and tossed it in the air. Star watched him toss and catch it, as if hoping he might throw it for her. Julian let his mind wander, trying to calculate how far they were from the island and guessing whether the treasure would be buried in a box or an old canvas sack.

Julian was jolted from his thoughts when he nearly tripped on Star and almost went flying to the ground. She stood as solid as a statue, right in his path. Julian tried to signal her to keep moving, but she ignored him. She scanned the tree line, her nose twitching and her head swinging around like crazy. Her whole body was tense, her tail stiff and alert. Bryan's head whipped back and forth, following her movements.

"What is it?" Bryan whispered.

Julian froze, trying to pick up whatever Star was sensing, but all he could hear were the leaves rustling in the breeze and Bryan's quick, nervous breathing. All he could see were insects skittering across the dry cornstalks. All he could smell was the earthy scent of maple trees and freshly turned dirt.

He tried to tell himself it was just a squirrel. Or

maybe Star sensed the farmer or a farmhand approaching. He imagined a tall man coming out of the woods with a hat pulled low over his eyes. Julian wished there was a place to hide so they wouldn't get caught and sent back across the field. But there was nothing around them except flattened cornstalks, and Star wasn't letting him get any closer to the woods.

What if there was something much worse than the farmer headed their way?

Star locked her eyes on a spot between two thick tree trunks off to their left. All the fur on her back stood up, and she growled low and fierce in her throat. Julian's heart pounded and his mind went blank with fear. Bryan's eyes were as round as Frisbees, and Julian knew that his friend was just as petrified as he was. Anything could be in those woods! But no matter how hard the boys strained their senses, they couldn't figure out what Star was growling at.

Until a twig snapped in the underbrush. Julian and Bryan jumped. With wide eyes, they slowly turned toward the sound. Julian wanted to whisper to Bryan that they should be ready to run, but his mouth felt like it was filled with cotton balls. He couldn't get any words out. Just as Star took a few steps forward, the huge head and shoulders of a black bear rose out of the thicket less than twenty feet away. A scream caught in Julian's throat. The ear of corn Bryan had been playing with dropped from his hand and hit the ground with a soft thud.

The bear turned to look at them. Julian had never seen a bear in the wild. He couldn't believe how massive its body was, filling the space between the trees. It had bits of twigs and leaves caught in its fur. The bear watched them with intelligent brown eyes. But Julian had no idea what it was thinking. He knew that if the bear came after them, they wouldn't be able to outrun it.

Julian frantically tried to remember whether you were supposed to run from a bear or curl into a ball or wave your arms around. He'd been a Cub Scout for only one summer before he'd had to start reading camp. He thought Bryan would know what to do, but when he glanced at his friend out of the corner of his eye, Bryan's face was blank with terror.

Star took another step forward, putting herself between the boys and the bear. She leaned forward aggressively. Her fur was so puffed out, she looked twice her size. She was tiny compared with the bear, but she clearly wasn't going to let that stop her. Star's growls turned into wild, protective barks that seemed to echo through the trees, bouncing from their trunks and across the field behind them. Julian and Bryan hadn't known she could make so much noise.

Julian held on to her leash with both hands. He didn't want to find out what would happen if she got away from him—and any closer to the bear.

The bear flicked its ears and raised its snout to sniff the air. As its nostrils twitched, its mouth opened just enough to reveal the tips of its teeth. It rocked back and stood up on its hind legs. Julian's breath caught in his throat. The animal was taller than anyone he knew —taller even than Bryan's dad. Its paws were as big as dinner plates, with claws like knives.

Star's barks got even louder and fiercer. Julian began to worry that she was making the bear mad, but in order to stop her, he would have to get her attention. To get her attention, he would have to move, and he was way too scared for that. Now he wished there *was* a farmer nearby to help them. But they were all alone.

The bear dropped back to all fours, shaking the bushes around it. Star growled, her ears back and pinned flat against her head. The bear took one long look at her, then swung its big head away and lumbered deeper into the woods. Julian hadn't realized that he'd been holding his breath, but then his chest began to hurt. He gasped for air and looked down at the dog, who stood in a fighter's stance as she watched the bear amble away. Star had saved them!

Star kept barking until the bear was out of sight. Still, once she quieted down, she stayed on high alert. The boys stood unmoving behind her. Finally she turned to look over her shoulder at Julian, her tongue out as she panted from all the excitement. Julian gave her a thumbs-up. If he had ten thumbs, it wouldn't have been enough to tell her what a good girl she was. He dropped to his knees, and she ran to him, nearly knocking him over. Bryan scratched her head while Julian petted her back, smoothing out the fur that had been standing on end. She leaned into Julian and licked his chin. Her tail was wagging so hard, she couldn't sit still. She even licked Bryan's hand and let him rub her belly. She was back to her sweet, gentle self, with no trace of the aggression she'd shown toward the bear.

Star shook out her fur and took a few steps toward the trees. She looked back at Julian and Bryan, as if telling them to move it along.

"We have to keep going before it gets dark," Bryan said. "Unless you want to turn back."

Julian's pulse hadn't quite returned to normal, but he felt safe with Star. He owed it to her to save the shelter. Julian got to his feet and faced the woods. He swallowed hard. "No way. We have to find the treasure."

Bryan nodded. They were in this together. The

boys looked at Star for any sign that something unexpected or dangerous was waiting for them beyond the tree line. She seemed calm and ready to explore the woods. They took a deep breath and crossed into the forest.

# ★ CHAPTER 17 ★

**Julian and Bryan** jumped at every little sound. Leaves rustled and twigs snapped all around them. The boys kept expecting the bear to reappear behind the next tree trunk. Star stayed close, but she didn't sound the alarm. Even so, as they headed deeper into the woods, they wondered if this was a good idea.

But it was too late to turn back. They were so close to Western Island and the buried treasure. The shelter animals needed them to find it. Star needed them to keep going.

The boys moved as quickly as they could along the trail. They had to get to Western Island before dusk —and they had to keep up with Star. The happy dog bounded over logs and poked her nose in the under-brush. She picked up a stick and carried it for a couple of minutes before abandoning it to sniff at a bug crawling up a tree trunk. It was her first time ever in the woods, and she was having a blast. Her excitement was just one more reason Julian was glad they'd brought her along.

"Bells!" Bryan said, smacking his palm against his forehead.

"What?" Julian turned to look at his friend and almost tripped over an exposed root in the trail.

"We should've brought bells or something to warn the bears," Bryan said. "I didn't know there were bears around Silver Lake. I didn't see any sign of them when I was here before."

"Me neither," Julian said.

"Maybe it's because we were here in the summer, when there are lots of people around," Bryan said. "The bears are probably too scared to come out, so they stay deeper in the woods where there are plenty of berries and stuff for them to eat."

That made sense to Julian. "So you mean that bear was probably as surprised to see us as we were to see it?"

"Exactly," Bryan said. "It was probably just out looking for food, getting ready for winter."

They looked at each other and swallowed hard. They hadn't just run into a bear—they'd run into a *hungry* bear. The boys suddenly realized how far they were from home. No one knew they were out here. It was just the two of them and Star.

Bryan laughed nervously. "We should keep talking to make sure we don't surprise the bear again."

"I'm starving," Julian said. He knew it wasn't much of a conversation starter, but now that they were out of danger, his stomach was grumbling loudly. "The bear won't come after our food, will it?"

"I think we're safe." Bryan dug the sandwiches out of his backpack. He handed one to Julian. "Besides, we've got Star to alert us."

Julian peeled back the foil around his sandwich. He tore off a piece of crust and gave it to Star as a reward. She gobbled it up. Julian trusted her to protect them, but to be on the safe side, he wanted to keep talking. He finished chewing his bite of sandwich and asked the first question that popped into his head. "So, do you have lots of dogs at home?"

Julian realized that he didn't know much about Bryan's life, except that he had just moved to town over the summer and his dad was the principal. Bryan had been coming to Julian's house to do homework. Julian had never gone to his, and Bryan and Principal Walter could live on a goat farm or in a castle and he wouldn't know it. Julian had a feeling that no one in their class knew much about the real Bryan.

"I can't have any animals." Bryan talked around a mouthful of sandwich. "My mom is super allergic. I have to change as soon as I get home from the shelter so I don't get fur all over the house."

"What about your brothers and sisters?" Julian asked.

"My little brother is allergic, too," Bryan said. "My older sister says she's going to get a cat when she goes to college, but I don't know how that's going to work, unless she never comes home."

"My brother used to pretend he had a dog when

we were little," Julian said. "Like, an invisible friend, except it was a puppy." He smiled at the memory of running around with Henry after his beloved pretend pet. Now that he and his brother barely talked, he sometimes forgot how much fun they used to have together.

Julian took a bite of his sandwich to cover his sadness. As much as he hated Henry's teasing, he missed hanging out with him.

"Are you going to adopt Star?" Bryan asked. "You have to, especially now that she saved our lives!"

"I don't know what would have happened without her," Julian said. "As soon as that bear appeared, I turned into a robot with a dead battery."

Bryan shook his head. "That's what I felt like, too. I thought we were prepared for everything. But I was *not* ready for a bear."

Julian went quiet for a long moment.

"I really want to adopt Star," he finally said. "I did even before we met the bear. But I don't know if my parents will let me. They're so busy, and they don't think I'm responsible enough for a dog."

"That's crazy," Bryan said. "You've done everything for Star."

"Yeah, but . . ." Julian paused, searching for the right words. How could he describe how hard it was for him to do everything his parents expected of him? He could tell Bryan that he knew they loved him and wanted what was best for him, but he didn't know how to say that he felt he was always disappointing them. Sometimes it seemed as if he spent his whole life being frustrated at school and then coming home and being frustrated with his homework—and being frustrat*ing* to his family. At least, that's what it had been like before he started volunteering and found Bryan and Star.

"It's easier at the shelter, where I can just focus on Star," Julian said. "But at home and in school, it's hard for me to keep up with everything. It's like when I saw that bear. I couldn't remember whether you're supposed to run or try to look big and scary. There were so many different thoughts going through my head that they got kind of jumbled together. And then it was over so fast, before I could untangle things. That's what it's like all the time."

Julian felt almost as vulnerable talking about what it was like in his head as he did facing the bear. But he knew that if anyone would understand, it would be Bryan. "I can't keep up with reading, so I just get farther and farther behind," Julian went on. "My parents try to help, but I don't think they really get what it's like. Especially since everything is so easy for my brother."

Bryan nodded thoughtfully as he crumpled the foil from his sandwich. "It must be hard with so many distractions at school."

"It is," Julian said. "But it feels like everyone else is able to keep up, so then all the teachers and my parents get frustrated with me."

"And then you land in detention with my dad," Bryan said.

Julian nodded. "He's not so bad, and I'm glad you and I got to hang out. But I hate getting in trouble all the time."

"I feel like I can't get in trouble." Bryan ducked his head. "My parents know a lot about dyslexia and have really helped me understand it. But I feel like I have to be perfect all the time since my dad's the principal."

"I never thought about that." Julian gave the last bite of his sandwich to Star. It hadn't occurred to him that Bryan worried about disappointing his parents, too.

"My parents expect me to set a good example and get good grades, even though it's harder for me than for most of the other kids," Bryan said. "I feel like all the teachers are constantly watching me to make sure I don't mess up."

Julian remembered how Ms. Hollin had singled Bryan out, and he knew that if he were in Bryan's place, he wouldn't be able to stand having teachers looking over his shoulder all the time. He hopped over a fallen log. "How does it feel to be breaking the rules?"

"It's a little scary," Bryan said. "But it's really nice to have a friend. Most of the time people just think I'm weird."

"People think I'm weird, too," Julian said, shrugging.

"We can be weird together," Bryan said, grinning.

Julian laughed. "Definitely."

Julian reached down to pet Star. Being there for each other had gotten the three of them this far. And up ahead, between the trees, he could see the sun sparkling off the lake. They were almost out of the woods.

# ★ CHAPTER 18 ★

**The trees thinned out,** and the dirt beneath their sneakers became soft and sandy. Star left a trail of pawprints as she pulled them toward the water. Julian and Bryan ducked beneath a low tree branch, and then they were standing on the shore of Silver Lake.

Julian, Bryan, and Star stared across the water. Julian couldn't believe they'd made it all the way out here on their own. Silver Lake was his favorite place in the world. He spent most of reading camp daydreaming about spending the weekend at the lake. When the winter snow turned to slush, Julian began counting the days until he'd be back here. Until he'd discovered the shelter and Star, this was the place where he'd felt most like himself.

It made sense that the shore of Silver Lake was where he'd find his first real treasure. And of all the lakes in Michigan, this was the one where Bryan had spent his summer, too. Everything was coming together. Julian could practically hear the gold calling to them.

Up ahead, a thin strip of land connected the woods to Western Island. The island's trees and the cloudless sky were reflected in the lake's surface like an upside-down world. In the summer, the illusion would be disturbed by boaters and swimmers, but at this time of year, there was no one else in sight. The sound of the water lapping gently at the shore was peaceful, but excitement brewed between the boys like a storm.

"Is that really it?" Bryan asked.

Julian nodded. "That's Western Island."

He and his dad had canoed here once from their campground on the other side of the lake. He'd almost lost his paddle when it got tangled in some reeds, but he'd managed to hang on to it without capsizing the boat. Then he'd spotted a small stretch of beach that his dad hadn't seen. He and his dad had gone ashore and eaten cherries and spent half the day exploring the woods, with no idea that there was buried treasure on the island. They might have walked right over it!

This was the first time Julian had approached Western Island from this side of the lake, but he recognized the curve of the shore from the old map. They were definitely in the right place. All they had to do now was follow the path they'd drawn on the map—from the land bridge to where the treasure should be waiting for them.

Bryan bounced on the balls of his feet, like he wished he could just leap across the water. "I can't believe we're so close," he said.

Julian took the map out of his backpack. He double-checked their route and landmarks. Then he looked at Bryan and grinned. "Let's go find the treasure."

Star sniffed at the ripples of water as they walked along the beach. When a small wave tumbled over her paws, she jumped back in surprise. Then she lowered her chest onto the wet sand, raised her rump high in the air, and gave a short bark at the lake. When the next wave rolled in, she snapped at it playfully. The boys laughed and ran with her to chase the never-ending waves.

They paused halfway across the land bridge, smiling and panting. Now that they were out from under the canopy of the woods, they could see the sky darkening from blue to purple as night crept closer. Bryan watched the orange line of the setting sun drop behind the island. "It's gotten really late," he said. "What do you think our parents will do when we're not home for dinner?"

"Hopefully they'll think I'm at your house and you're at mine," Julian said. "And hopefully no one will call to make sure."

"I don't know if my dad will fall for that. He's probably already tried to call me." Bryan dug his phone out of his backpack. When he checked the screen, his face clouded with worry. "I don't have any signal out here."

Julian unzipped the small pocket on his backpack and checked his phone. "Me either." He quickly stuffed the phone back into his bag. "It's okay," he said, trying to sound like there was nothing to worry about. "We know exactly where we are, and we have Star to keep us safe."

Bryan looked across the water, back the way they'd come. "What if Ms. Khan knows that Star's gone by now? She'll be really worried."

A pang of guilt squeezed Julian's chest even as he watched Star play. "It will all be worth it."

"Yeah, I know." Bryan didn't sound convinced, but Julian felt in his bones that they were close to digging up life-changing loot. He wondered what half a million dollars in gold looked like. Or how much it weighed. He hoped they'd be able to fit it all in their backpacks. They might have to leave their supplies behind and come back for them another day.

They reached the far end of the land bridge and passed a large rock formation that looked like a giant's boot. Everything was exactly as the map said it would be. There was the tree with a trunk curved like a pointing finger. And the bend in the trail, like a slithering snake. Julian was so excited he didn't have room in his thoughts to worry about whether he'd get into trouble for all the rules they'd broken today.

They reached a small clearing that was far enough inland to conceal people burying a treasure, but not so far that it would've been hard to get there quickly. Julian and Bryan looked around for the telltale sign: two trees growing so close together that their trunks crossed in an X, marking the spot. They figured that the bandits had needed a way to find the spot again, and the twisted trees — neatly drawn on the map — were the perfect landmark. But all the trees stood tall and straight.

Bryan wandered across the clearing, his brow furrowed. Julian felt doubt slipping over him like a blanket. Maybe they'd been wrong about one of the clues left behind by the thieves and other treasure hunters. He triple-checked the map. He knew exactly where they were on the island. He ran his finger over the landmarks they'd passed on the way to the clearing. He was certain this was the right place. Those trees had to be here somewhere.

"Over here!" Bryan shouted.

Julian and Star ran over to where Bryan was crouched close to the ground.

"Look how close these stumps are to each other," Bryan said. "You can see them kind of leaning toward each other. I think someone cut down the trees."

"They look like they're sharing a secret," Julian said.

"A secret treasure." Bryan's face broke into a huge smile.

"Okay—where do we start digging?" Julian asked.

Bryan dropped his backpack and took out a trowel. He paced around the stumps, studying the ground. He tugged at his hair and narrowed his eyes. Then he used the edge of the trowel to draw a big X in the dirt between the stumps. "It should be right here."

Julian and Bryan knelt down and began scraping at the ground with their garden tools. Once they'd loosened the crust, they used the trowels and their hands to scoop dirt away. It had gotten dark enough on the island that they could only make out the shapes of the stumps and trees around them. But they didn't need to see what they were doing. They just needed to dig.

Star poked her snout between them. She whined and licked at Julian's face. He paused to scratch her chin, then got back to work. He didn't have a hand signal to tell her what was going on, but once they found the gold and she was safe, he'd give her a million belly rubs.

Star gave an impatient bark. Then she wriggled her way between Julian and Bryan and began digging at the hole with her paws, flinging dirt everywhere. The boys shielded their faces from the flying dirt. They shifted around to get out of Star's way and scooped the loosened dirt out of the hole as she dug. Together, the three of them kept digging and scooping. With every handful and pawful of dirt, it felt like they were getting closer to striking gold.

Julian's fingers brushed against something hard. He tapped Star's shoulder and gave her the signal to sit. She lay down instead, her front paws and head hanging over the edge of the hole. Bryan sat back on his knees, his eyes wide in the growing darkness. Julian was pretty sure he'd hit a rock. But his hand was shaking as he stuck his trowel into the hole to loosen the rock from the dirt. The tip of the blade hit a flat, solid surface. Julian reached down to wipe away a layer of dirt, revealing the smooth top of an old rusted metal box.

# ★ CHAPTER 19 ★

**Julian and Bryan** scraped the dirt away from the edges of the box, trying to loosen it enough to lift it out of the hole. It wouldn't move, even after they had all four corners of the top exposed. It had been buried for a hundred years, with countless people and animals walking over it, tamping down the dirt. Julian hoped it wasn't so packed in there that it would take them another hundred years to dig it out.

It was getting harder and harder to see what they were doing. Something rustled in the woods near the clearing. Julian glanced at Star. She wasn't worried at all. She was focused on the hole in the ground, her head tilted, as if she too were impatient to find out what was in the box. Bryan stopped digging. He flicked on his flashlight and nervously swept the beam across the trees. Julian could tell that his friend was spooked by being out in the wild so late. He wondered if the bear had gone to bed. But now that Julian's hands were on the treasure, nothing would stop him from bringing it back.

"Come on, get it out of there," Bryan urged him, aiming the beam of his flashlight onto the box.

"I'm trying!" Julian dug and scraped. His arms were getting tired and his hands were caked with dirt.

Julian finally dislodged enough dirt to wiggle the box around. He got a grip on the edges and freed it from the earth, hefting it awkwardly up and onto the sandy ground. It looked like it had been made of a dark greenish metal, but now it was covered in dirt and rust. Julian stood up and walked in a circle around the box, studying it from all sides. It was smaller than the treasure chest he'd imagined—a little smaller than his dad's toolbox—and a lot lighter. Maybe it was stuffed with cash instead of gold bricks or coins. The bills would be old and brittle, but he was sure the bank would still take them, as long as they hadn't been eaten by bugs. Maybe they'd even be worth more, like his grandpa's coin collection.

Julian wiped his sweaty palms on his jeans, squatted down, and reached for the thin metal latch on the front of the metal container.

It wouldn't budge. It was rusted shut.

Julian tried to pry it open with the butt of his flashlight. But the latch was frozen in place.

"Let me try." Bryan set down his flashlight and took the box from Julian. He placed it on the ground and banged a rock against the rusty latch until it broke off. The dented lid gaped like an open mouth. Julian and Bryan looked at each other. They took a deep breath and opened the lid the rest of the way. The weathered hinges creaked in the quiet clearing. The boys leaned forward to peer inside.

It was empty.

Julian picked up the box and shook it. Maybe there was a small diamond or ruby left behind in one of the corners. But nothing rattled. He reached into the box and swept his fingertips across every surface. He felt for a false bottom, like he'd seen in a movie once. He held the box upside down and shook it. Nothing came out. Not even a money-eating beetle. He let the empty box fall to the ground. Star sniffed at it and quickly lost interest.

Bryan shone his flashlight into the box. He leaped to his feet. He checked where they'd been sitting. He searched the hole and all around the stumps. Star chased the beam as he moved it over the ground. Then he put the flashlight away and pushed both hands into his hair. "Nothing! There's nothing here!"

"That's impossible." Julian picked up the metal box again, as if something might have magically appeared inside. It was still empty. Everything they'd been through had been for nothing. He didn't want to believe it. They needed this treasure. They couldn't go back empty-handed. He'd never be allowed out of the house again, and Star would be sent off to a distant shelter. This felt like his biggest failure ever.

"There has to be a different one. This isn't it. It's just someone's old lunch box or something. I bet if we keep digging . . ." Julian trailed off. Deep down, he knew this was it. He and Bryan had put their heads together and figured out where the long-lost treasure was hidden. His map had led them right to it. Except someone else had gotten there first.

"Why didn't whoever found it post it online?" Bryan said. "It's not fair to everyone else!"

"Maybe the bandits came back for it and never told anyone. Maybe it hasn't been here for a hundred years." Julian imagined thieves sneaking back into these woods, digging up their gold, then burying the empty box as a big joke. He was crushed. They'd come all this way and risked everything with Star for nothing. The treasure wasn't real. They'd never even had a chance.

Finding the box empty was almost worse than not finding it at all. Both boys' faces were smudged with dirt, and their shoulders were slumped with disappointment as they trudged back over the land bridge, leaving Western Island and the empty box behind them. They hadn't reburied it or filled in the hole. If any other treasure hunters came along after them, they'd know it was a dead end right away. When they got to the opposite shore, Bryan stopped short. The woods were pitch-black. "Is there another way?" he asked. "Maybe one without bears?"

Julian wasn't looking forward to the trek through the dark woods either. He was exhausted. Even without the treasure, his backpack seemed heavier than when they'd started. He wished he was already at home in his warm pajamas. He took out his flashlight and checked the map. "We can cut through this edge of the woods. Then it looks like there are old railroad tracks we can follow back to the main road. This should keep us off that farm, too."

"Let's go that way," Bryan said.

The three of them started walking home in silence. The snacks were long gone, and the boys hadn't thought to bring jackets. They zipped their hoodies against the cool night breeze. It would be long after dark when they got home, and they knew they'd both be in big trouble. But they were so cold, hungry, and disappointed that they couldn't even get upset about being grounded for the rest of their lives. Julian just hoped he'd be allowed to see Star again. He reached down to pet her soft, warm fur. She rubbed against his leg, then pulled ahead, her tail wagging. As far as she was concerned, they were still on a great adventure.

They found the train tracks right where Julian's map said they would be. The moon had started to rise, casting a warm light over the rails, which seemed to stretch on forever. They were overgrown with weeds, and the wooden ties looked old and split. They walked down the middle of the tracks toward home.

The boys didn't talk much, as if all conversation had been drained out of them. Star could tell that they were bummed, and she nuzzled their hands as if trying to cheer them up.

After they'd been walking for what felt like an hour, they stopped at the edge of an old steel rail bridge that carried the tracks across the river. According to Julian's map, the road was just on the other side of it.

Bryan paused to take a drink of water. Julian took out his water bottle, too, and offered some to Star in her bowl. But Star wouldn't even look at the water. She seemed agitated, pacing back and forth. Julian understood. He was eager to get home too.

The boys put their water bottles away and surveyed the journey ahead. The bridge was just wide enough for one train to pass. There was no walkway. They would have to walk right down the tracks.

"What if a train comes while we're on the bridge?" Bryan asked quietly.

Julian swallowed hard. "It looks so old—do you think any trains still go over it?"

Bryan shook his head. "I really hope not."

With a solemn nod, Julian stepped out onto the bridge and began to make his way across. Star trotted close by his side, but the farther along they got, the more the dog tried to pull them back the way they had come.

"I think she's afraid of crossing," Julian said over his shoulder to Bryan, who marched right behind him.

"That makes two of us," Bryan said. "Do you think this is safe?"

"Just be careful where you step," Julian said. "I'm sure it's fine."

Bryan craned his neck to look over the bridge railing without getting too close. Moonlight shone on the dark water churning far below. "It's a long way down."

Julian stepped carefully over a big gap in the wood beneath their feet. Star leaped gracefully over it, but as soon as she landed, she froze. Julian stopped short, and Bryan nearly bumped into him.

"Hang on." Julian squatted down and signaled to Star. She came to him for a second, but then tried to pull him back in the other direction. When he didn't budge, she looked him square in the eye, held his gaze, and whined, as if she were desperate to tell him something.

Julian sighed. "I know it's scary," he said soothingly. "But it's the only way home. I promise we'll be over the bridge before you know it."

"The sooner the better," Bryan said. "Come on, Star—I don't like this any more than you do."

Julian wrapped the leash around his hand so he could keep Star close. She walked with him, but her ears were pinned back against her head and she kept glancing around with big, worried eyes. Julian gave her lots of thumbs-up signs to encourage her. He thought about his grandpa and Liberty and all the scary situations they must have gone through together. "You're being so brave, girl. Look—we're almost halfway there."

"Julian?" This time, Bryan had stopped short.

"Wha—" Before Julian could get the rest of the sentence out, he felt something that made him fall silent. It was . . . what was it? He focused on the strange sensation rising up from his feet—a faint vibration through the soles of his shoes. At first it felt like pins and needles, but then it became more of a rumble than a tingle. He and Bryan locked eyes, both boys realizing what was happening at the exact same time. They suddenly understood what Star had been trying to tell them: She wasn't afraid of the bridge. *She was afraid of the train!*

"Run!" Julian and Bryan screamed in unison.

The train was getting closer. They heard it clearly in the distance, and they raced ahead as quickly as they could, leaping over bumpy boards and missing planks. Star led the way. She might not be able to hear it, but she'd felt it coming long before they did. The rumbling beneath their feet grew more intense. Julian glanced over his shoulder and saw the moonlight glinting off the front of the train, which was now bearing down on them in the darkness. The engine roared through the woods behind them.

In another second, it would reach the bridge. They weren't going to make it across in time.

Julian kept his eyes on the tracks, too scared to look behind him again. The rails vibrated as the train got closer and closer, and soon the whole bridge felt as if it were being shaken by a giant. Right behind Julian, Bryan stumbled over a crack and barely managed to keep his footing. Julian reached out to steady his friend. With one hand holding the leash and the other on Bryan's arm, he pulled Bryan forward, both of them breathing hard. They had to keep moving, even though there was no way they could outrun a train. Maybe Star could if she wasn't on her leash, but she didn't try to pull away. She wasn't going to leave the boys behind.

Suddenly Star stopped short, and to Julian's horror, she dove through a gaping hole in the wood at their feet, disappearing from view. Julian's heart leaped into his throat. Where was she? Did Star just jump into the water? But the bridge was way too high—she would never survive! He looked up at Bryan, who was staring with wide, shocked eyes at the place where Star had disappeared. Behind him, Julian saw the train barreling toward them, a huge black shadow against the night sky.

Julian's mind spiraled through a thousand terrified and heartbreaking thoughts at once, but one was more urgent than all the others: They had to keep moving. But no way would he leave without Star. He looked down at the leash wrapped around his wrist, and that's when it hit him—the leash hadn't gone taut! Star hadn't fallen—she had to be right below them!

"Down!" Julian shouted at Bryan. With not a half second to waste, the boys dropped down into a gap in the boards just wide enough for them to slip through. They landed on the wide steel beams of the trestle below and crawled over to where Star crouched, waiting for them.

They had followed her blindly, trusting her with their lives for the second time that day, and they had made it to safety just in time. The steel shook around them as the train thundered overhead. Julian felt like his heart was beating louder than the train itself. He tried not to think about how old and rickety the bridge felt. Bryan covered his ears with his hands.

Star panted as she cowered against Julian. She might not be able to hear the train, but she was feeling it as it passed — it was as if the whole world were rumbling around them. Julian wrapped his arms around the trembling dog to comfort her. His hand touched something wet, and Star flinched. Julian looked down. In the bars of moonlight shining through the gaps in the boards above, he could see that the pattern on her back had changed. The white fur on Star's side was soaked and matted with blood.

# ★ CHAPTER 20 ★

**Julian held Star** as close as he could without hurting her. Between the booming train and his worry that she was badly hurt, Julian was shaking too. She pressed against him, whining softly. In the cramped space below the tracks, it was impossible to get a better look. All he knew was that she was in pain.

The last car of the train passed overhead, sucking the air along with it. The sound of the churning wheels faded quickly, and they were left in silence. Julian sat still, his arm around Star, until her shaking—and the pounding of his heart—began to subside.

Julian looked around. The opening they'd dived into to escape the train was a narrow, awkward space set between two steel pillars. It was barely enough room to hold them all, and it was dangerous in its own right. There were shards of broken wood and bent steel rods scattered around. It was a miracle they had made it down there safely. Or mostly had. Not Star.

"She's bleeding," Julian said.

"Is she okay?" Bryan gasped.

"I think so. But we need to get her out of here."

Bryan stood up as much as he could in the low space and poked his head out by the tracks, like a groundhog making sure the coast was clear. He scrambled up the trestle and lay down on the walkway above, then reached back down for Star. Julian held the dog up to Bryan and climbed up after her.

Star cried out as Julian carried her, as gently as he could, to solid ground at the end of the bridge. Each howl pierced through Julian. They set her down in the grass, and she took a few steps before lying down with a whimper.

"She's really hurt." Julian's voice was shaking. "She's bleeding pretty bad."

"She must have cut herself on one of the beams or something." Bryan knelt beside Star and took a red nylon pouch out of his backpack. His first-aid kit had bandages, gauze, and little packets of antibiotic cream. He shone his flashlight on Star, but with her thick fur darkened by blood, they couldn't tell exactly where the injury was or how badly she was hurt. They didn't think any of the bandages were big enough to help her, and they didn't know how they'd get the gauze to stick to her fur anyway. All they knew for sure was that they had to get her to the vet.

"Maybe we can call for help." Bryan took out his phone. He stared at the screen longer than necessary before putting it away, looking defeated. "Still no signal. We must be too far from town."

"We need to carry her." Julian took off his sweatshirt and wrapped it around the shaking dog. The cool night air raised goose bumps on his bare arms. Bryan put away his useless first-aid kit and helped Julian tie the sweatshirt around Star. As carefully as he could, Julian lifted her into his arms and started walking.

She was so much lighter than he expected. With all her energy and personality, he'd thought she'd weigh a ton, but it was like carrying a basket of laundry.

"You'll be okay," he whispered into her soft ear. Even though she couldn't hear him, she felt his breath and whined in response.

Bryan kept the flashlight trained on the ground in front of Julian so he wouldn't trip on anything. They made sure to walk as far away from the train tracks as they could without losing sight of them. The tracks felt unlucky now. The whole adventure had turned unlucky. Bryan kept up a steady chatter about trains, warning Julian about rocks and reassuring him that they were close to the road. Bryan insisted that he could hear cars in the distance. Julian wasn't sure he believed him, but he appreciated Bryan's encouragement as he carried Star through the night. Bryan even made sure to give Star plenty of thumbs-ups and scratches on the head to help comfort her.

"She's shivering," Julian said, his voice cracking with emotion. It was heartbreaking to think that Star was suffering right there in his arms and there was nothing he could do about it. He could feel her blood soaking through his sweatshirt. Bryan stopped walking and sacrificed his own sweatshirt. Julian set Star down so they could wrap the second layer around her, bundling her up as best as they could.

"Do you want me to carry her?" Bryan offered.

"No. I've got her." Julian shook out the tired muscles of his arms. He lifted Star and kept going.

"We're not far," Bryan promised, shining the flashlight ahead of them.

Julian began to doubt his estimate of how far it was from the bridge to the road. He was really good at reading maps, but maybe he'd gotten it wrong this time. Maybe they weren't anywhere near the road and would just keep walking until they reached Canada. He was just about to stop to check the map and rest his arms when he heard the soft whoosh of tires on pavement. A tiny bit of hope flared inside him, giving him the energy to cross the last fifty feet through the underbrush. They'd made it out of the wilderness. They could get help for Star now.

Julian gently laid the dog in the grass by the side

of the road. He sat beside her, stroking the fur on her head. Her breaths were quick and shallow, her eyes half closed. Julian wished he had a way to tell her she'd be okay. Even though he wasn't sure if she was really seeing him, he gave her a shaky thumbs-up as he fought back tears.

Bryan unzipped his backpack and took out his phone. Now that they were close enough to town for it to pick up a signal, the phone was buzzing with message notifications from his parents and Ms. Khan. Bryan ignored all the messages and called his dad.

Before Star got hurt, the boys would have walked the whole way home, putting off the moment when they'd have to face Ms. Khan and their parents. But Star couldn't wait that long. They had to get her to the vet fast. They weren't worried anymore about how much trouble they'd be in. They were just worried about saving Star.

Principal Walter sped to the emergency veterinary hospital. The questions would come later, but for now they rode in anxious silence. Julian sat in the back seat, with Star's head in his lap. The only other time he'd been in this car was during detention when Mr. Walter had taken him to the shelter for the first time. He'd felt so frustrated and out of place that day.

So much in Julian's life was different then. He hadn't even met Star yet. He'd never really talked to Bryan. And that was the last time he'd gotten detention. Now he finally felt like he knew who he was and where he belonged. But none of that would matter if he lost Star.

When they got to the animal hospital, a vet tech met them at the curb and rushed Star inside. One second she was draped over Julian's lap and the next she was gone. He sat in the back seat, feeling cold and alone.

Principal Walter held open the back door. "Come on. Let's go wait inside."

Julian and Bryan sat in chairs in the waiting room, staring at the door to the treatment rooms. They wanted to know the instant the vet came out with any news. The receptionist brought them Styrofoam cups filled with hot cocoa made from powdered mix in the break room. Principal Walter found a couple of oversize school sweatshirts in his trunk. Even with the warm clothes and hot cocoa, Julian couldn't stop shivering. He took one sip and set the cocoa on a table that was covered with dog magazines. His stomach was too upset for him to drink.

Julian didn't like the quiet in the waiting room. He wanted it to be more like the hospital shows his parents sometimes watched, with a flurry of doctors and nurses shouting to one another and machines beeping in the background. He wanted the room to be as chaotic as he felt inside.

Whatever they were doing to try to save Star was happening behind that closed door. No one came out to talk to them. No one would even tell them if Star was going to live or die. She'd lost a lot of blood and had been very weak by the time they'd gotten to the hospital.

Julian didn't know how long they sat there in silence before his parents arrived. They rushed into the waiting room in a swirl of cold air and anxious energy. Principal Walter intercepted them at the door and took them to the opposite side of the room. The adults talked in voices too low for the boys to hear. Julian kept his eyes locked on the door. He couldn't bear to see the anger and disappointment on his parents' faces.

Slouching in his chair as his parents approached, he wished he could disappear. Or zoom back in time to earlier that day, before he and Bryan had decided to take Star from the shelter. Maybe even before they'd decided to go on their stupid treasure hunt. He'd done the most thoughtless, irresponsible thing ever. He deserved whatever punishment his parents gave him.

Julian's parents squatted in front of him so he had no choice but to meet their eyes. In the chair next to him, Bryan squirmed and looked away. He'd have to deal with his own punishment later.

Julian's mom squeezed his hand. "We're glad you're safe, Julian. That's the most important thing."

"But Star's not safe," he said.

"She's getting the best care possible." His mom spoke quietly, trying to comfort him. Julian didn't want to be comforted.

"It's all my fault," Julian said. "She's hurt because of me."

"We know you didn't mean for this to happen," his dad said.

"But I made bad choices," Julian insisted.

"You did," his dad agreed. "We're disappointed in you for taking Star without permission. And for not telling us where you were going. And for breaking your curfew. Okay, for a lot of things—but the point is, you know what you did was wrong."

"It's fine if you ground me forever," Julian said. He didn't mind the idea. He'd spend the rest of his life in his room if he knew Star was going to be okay.

"Right now, we just want to make sure Star gets better," his mom said. "We'll figure out the rest later."

His parents' grim expressions remained fixed. Julian could feel how worried they'd been about him. His chest was heavy with guilt, and he was relieved when they finally walked across the room to sit down next to Principal Walter.

"That wasn't so bad," Bryan whispered.

"That was worse than bad," Julian muttered. "I should be in trouble. I ruined everything."

"It's not your fault that Star got hurt," Bryan said.

Julian turned to face Bryan. "It's all my fault! I'm always doing stuff without thinking."

"Not this time," Bryan said. "I was there, too, remember? We had a plan. I was prepared. I thought I was ready for anything, but I wasn't at all."

Julian crossed his arms and shook his head. "It was my stupid idea to chase after the treasure."

"It wasn't stupid." Bryan shook his head. "We couldn't have known this was going to happen. But we're in this together. You, me, and Star."

Julian knew that his friend was trying to make him feel better, but Bryan's words only made him more miserable. Bryan never got in trouble. He probably had never broken a single rule before today. Now Julian had made him break all of them. And Bryan could've gotten seriously hurt. Julian's crazy ideas had put both Star and Bryan in danger.

Ms. Khan burst into the animal hospital. She went straight to the reception desk. "I'm here for Star."

"The doctor is working on her now. She'll be out with news as soon as Star is stable." The receptionist offered a sympathetic smile and nodded toward the chairs where Julian, Bryan, and their parents waited.

"But she's going to be okay, right?" Ms. Khan asked.

"I'm sorry," the receptionist said. "I don't have any more information than you do until Dr. Everett comes out."

Her answer made Julian feel hollow. He'd needed to hear her say *yes, of course Star will be okay.* What if Star didn't make it? What if . . . Julian couldn't let himself finish the thought.

Ms. Khan turned from the reception desk. She glanced around, as if she hadn't noticed the crowded waiting room. Her gaze landed on Julian and Bryan for a long, uncomfortable moment. Julian couldn't tell what she was thinking. He pulled the sleeves of the oversize sweatshirt over his hands, as if he could disappear into it.

Ms. Khan didn't say anything to the boys or their

parents. She didn't sit down. She just paced back and forth across the waiting room.

This couldn't have been further from the scene Julian had imagined—he and Bryan safely returning Star and presenting Ms. Khan with enough gold to save the shelter. Julian knew he should say something, but he didn't know where to start. He'd let Ms. Khan down. She probably wouldn't let him anywhere near the shelter again, for however long it remained open.

Julian was about to turn to Bryan, hoping he'd know what to say. But before he had the chance, the door swung open and a tired-looking woman was striding toward them, a stethoscope draped around her neck. The veterinarian had news.

# ★ CHAPTER 21 ★

**Dr. Everett strode** into the waiting room, serious and solemn. Julian and Bryan leaped to their feet. She wore dark blue scrubs with colorful, playful dogs printed all over the top. Julian stared at the cheerful pattern, but it didn't make him feel any better. He tugged anxiously at the cuffs of his borrowed sweatshirt. The vet didn't start talking until everyone had gathered around her. "Star has a deep cut on her side, but I was able to clean it out," she said. "She'll have to stay here for a few days to make sure she doesn't get an infection. After that, she'll need to rest for a few weeks. Her wound will have to be kept clean, but she'll be okay."

Julian sank back into his chair. Relief made his legs

turn to jelly. His mom came over and put a hand on his shoulder. Bryan and his father hugged each other.

"Thank you," Ms. Khan said, her eyes welling up with tears.

"Star's a lucky dog," the vet said. Julian thought a lucky dog wouldn't have to get stitched up at all. But then he looked around the waiting room at all the people who were worried about Star, and he guessed she was pretty lucky to have so many people who loved her.

"Can I see her?" Julian asked.

The vet shook her head. "Not tonight. She needs to rest. But you can come back tomorrow if your parents say it's okay."

Julian looked at them hopefully. His parents exchanged a glance.

"Why don't you go wait for us in the car?" his mom said. "We'll be out in a minute."

Julian's heart sank. What if his parents decided he could never see Star again? He knew he'd messed up, but he needed her in his life. Still, right now, all he could do was what he was told. He said goodbye to Bryan and thanked Principal Walter for picking them up. He mumbled that he was sorry to Ms. Khan. He knew it wasn't nearly enough, but he was all out of words.

Julian was totally drained from the emotional rollercoaster of the day, but he couldn't sit still. He paced laps around the car, hoping the cool night air would calm him down. Even though the vet had said Star was going to be okay, adrenaline still pulsed through his body, leaving him restless and worried.

He looked at the clinic building. Rectangles of light spilled from the windows and splashed across the grass. He wondered if Star was behind one of them. He hoped she had a cozy blanket. He hoped she wasn't scared being in a strange place where no one knew her hand signals. He wanted to go inside and show the staff how to talk to her. He wanted them to give her lots of thumbs-ups, so she'd know she was a good girl and none of this was her fault. He wanted to tell them that she liked to be scratched behind the ears. But now wasn't the time to disobey his parents. They'd told him to wait outside, and that's what he had to do.

Way too many minutes later, his parents came

out. Before they even reached the car, Julian ran up to them. "I promise I'll never do anything like this ever again. I more than promise—I swear I won't. I know I messed up. But you have to let me see Star again!"

His voice broke, and tears pricked at his eyes before spilling down his cheeks.

His dad crossed his arms and studied the asphalt for a moment before looking Julian directly in the eye. "What you did was very serious, Jules. It's not just about Star. You and Bryan could've gotten hurt. You made choices that put you all in danger."

Julian looked down at his shoes, unable to hold his dad's gaze.

"That's why you can only go to school and the shelter for the rest of this semester," his dad said.

Julian gaped at his parents. "I'm still allowed to go to the shelter?"

"No more treasure hunting. No hanging out with Bryan outside of school as long as you're both grounded," his dad continued. "And we expect good grades."

"No more detentions," his mom added. "We'll get

you a tutor if you need extra help, but you'll complete all your homework."

"But I can go back to the shelter?" Julian repeated. It seemed too good to be true. "I can see Star again?"

"We just talked to Ms. Khan, and we agreed that the best way for you to learn to take more responsibility is to keep working at the shelter."

"She must be so mad at me," Julian said, his voice quiet with shame.

"You did break the rules, and you'll have to regain her trust." His mom reached for his hand and gave it a squeeze. "But we all know that you and Bryan meant well. Honey, it's just that you tried to help in the least practical way."

"The shelter is going to be shut down, and we had to stop it—" Julian was trying to explain himself, but the plan and his emotions were getting all jumbled inside of him. "It was the only way I could think of."

Julian thought back to how sure he'd been that there was hidden gold out there, just waiting for him and Bryan to find it. Now that it was over, he realized how ridiculous it had been to chase after buried treasure. He might as well have wished for a pot of gold at the end of a rainbow or finding an old lamp with a genie in it to grant him three wishes.

"None of us want the shelter to close." Dad put an arm around Julian's shoulders. "We love that you're so passionate about Star and the other animals, but you became so focused on trying to help that you couldn't see what was reasonable."

Julian hung his head. The plan had made so much sense when he and Bryan had set out that day—he was sure they'd thought of everything. Saving Star and the shelter had become so important to him that the thought of losing them made him leap into action. He'd focused in a way he never had before, but now he saw that it was too much, as if he'd crawled into a tunnel and the rest of the world had disappeared.

Julian sighed. "I never thought I could be *too* focused on something. I couldn't think about anything except Star. I couldn't even see how crazy the idea was."

"Ms. Khan told us how good you've been for her," his mom said. "We know you can do so much when you put your amazing mind to it."

"I can't give up on her," Julian said.

"No one is giving up on Star or the shelter," his dad said. "We'll help you figure out another way to try to help, okay?"

Julian nodded. He leaned into his dad, and his mom wrapped her arms around both of them. Julian sagged against them. For once, he didn't have a single idea of what to do next.

"One more thing." His mom ruffled his hair. "Once the vet says it's okay, you can bring Star home."

Julian tilted his head back to see her face. He couldn't believe his ears. "Wait . . . what?"

Both of his parents were trying not to smile, but their eyes crinkled at the corners.

"We can see how much you love her," his dad said. "And she's been as good for you as you've been for her. You're much better when you're together."

"What you did today was beyond irresponsible," his mom said. "But Ms. Khan says—and we agree —that the best place for Star to heal is with you. And with our family."

Julian hugged his parents even tighter, burying

his face in the fleece of his dad's jacket. He couldn't stop smiling, even as mixed-up tears spilled down his cheeks. His mind swam in a swirling current of exhaustion, guilt, and love. He and Star belonged together. But he'd almost lost her forever today. He made a million silent promises to Star, his parents, Ms. Khan, and Bryan that he'd be much more responsible from now on. Nothing had gone the way he'd expected, but Star was going to get better. She would finally be part of his family.

# ★ CHAPTER 22 ★

**Julian and Bryan** sat in the office after school, waiting for Mr. Walter. Other kids shot curious glances through the big window, wondering what the two boys had done to land themselves in the chairs outside the principal's office. Bryan sat with a book open on his lap, trying to ignore the stares. Julian felt like he was on the wrong side of a tank at the aquarium. He knew the other kids would tease them if they heard about the failed treasure hunt. He'd probably get a pirate nickname that would stick for the rest of his life.

Principal Walter finally emerged from his office and drove the boys to the shelter, where their bikes were still stashed in the bushes from the day before.

Bryan slung a leg over his bike and mumbled, "See you tomorrow."

"Yeah. Good luck," Julian said. Bryan's parents had decided that his punishment was to do chores around the house before he could go back to the shelter. Today he was supposed to rake up all the leaves in the Walters' yard — and the Walters had huge trees.

"You too," Bryan said, and he rode off toward home.

Julian gripped his handlebars, lingering by the edge of the parking lot. He desperately wanted to hop on his bike and pedal as fast he could to see Star, but he had to make things better with Ms. Khan first. He took a deep breath and wheeled his bike to its usual spot around the side of the shelter.

Ms. Khan wasn't in the lobby or her office. That part of the shelter felt like a ghost town. If it weren't for the sound of barking dogs carrying down the hall from the kennels, Julian might have worried that the shelter had been shut down overnight.

He found Ms. Khan in the kitchen, up to her elbows in sudsy water and dirty dog food bowls. Her shoulders were slumped, and a few strands of hair had escaped from her usually neat ponytail. Julian hadn't even seen her face, but he could tell she was exhausted. And at least part of it was his fault. A knot of guilt lodged in his throat as he walked over to her.

"I can do the dishes," he said, picking up a dishtowel. "Or laundry. Or scoop kennels. Whatever you need."

"What are you doing here?" she asked without looking at him.

Julian took the dripping bowl from her hands and toweled it off. He didn't know how else to let her know how sorry he was. He imagined how scared she must have been to find Star missing from her kennel.

"I'm so sorry. I'm going to make it up to you and show you that you can trust me again," Julian said.

Ms. Khan turned off the faucet and took the towel from Julian to dry her hands. He picked up another towel and twisted it nervously. Even though his parents had told him that Ms. Khan would forgive him, he expected her to tell him to get lost and never come back.

Ms. Khan let out a long sigh before speaking. "I know you and Bryan were trying to help," she said, setting the towel on the counter. "But what I meant was, what are you doing *here?*"

Julian swallowed, realization dawning on him.

Ms. Khan pointed at the door. "Now go visit Star. I've got things under control here, but she needs you. You're the only one who really knows how to communicate with her."

Julian didn't need to be told twice.

The receptionist at the animal hospital greeted Julian when he burst into the lobby. He was breathing hard from biking as fast as he could from the shelter.

"Ms. Khan called and said you were on your way," she said. She pushed back her chair and waved Julian to follow her down the hall. "I have to warn you, Star's pretty sleepy from her medication."

"Is she doing okay?" Julian asked.

"She's a little afraid, but she's very sweet," the receptionist said. "She'll be more than ready to get out of here in a few days."

Julian opened his mouth to ask if anyone was using hand signals with her or petting the spot she liked behind her left ear, but as they passed through a swinging door, he sucked in his breath. There was Star, looking so small and frail in her metal cage. She lay on her side, a giant plastic cone shielding her head so she couldn't chew on the huge bandage wrapped around her middle. When she saw Julian, she lifted her head and whined, her tail swishing against the wall of the cage.

"I'll leave you two alone," the receptionist said. "Try not to get her too excited. I'll be up front if you need anything."

Julian sat on the floor and opened the cage. Fighting tears, he reached inside the plastic cone to scratch Star behind the ear. He could barely bring himself to look at her bandage. He didn't want to imagine what was beneath it or how much it must have hurt. There was a sharp antiseptic smell in the room. Everything around them was stainless steel, white floors, tubes, and bandages. They were a million miles from the excitement and fresh air of Silver Lake.

Star turned her head to lick his wrist. He wished he had a hand signal that could explain everything to her. He wanted to tell her how sorry he was and that everything was going to be different from now on.

"You'll be better soon," he promised. "And then you get to come home."

Star nuzzled against Julian's hand. He lightly stroked the soft fur on top of her head. He told her all about his house and her new family. He said he couldn't wait for her to meet Grandpa and that he'd probably be able to teach her all kinds of cool stuff. He apologized over and over again. Star's eyes slowly closed.

Julian would've liked to set up camp next to the cage and stay with her until it was time to bring her home. He wished he'd brought a sleeping bag. He could order pizza for dinner and feed her the crusts and slices of pepperoni. The receptionist was so nice. He thought she might let him stay, but he had to leave in an hour. He needed to finish his homework and get to bed early so he'd wake up the first time his alarm clock went off. He had to be on time for school and make sure his laundry was in the basket before he left the house.

He had to be perfect, to make sure his parents didn't change their minds about Star. But it wasn't easy. Julian was working harder than he ever had before. He wrote down all his assignments in a notebook each day and checked them off as he completed them, making sure he didn't miss a single one. He downloaded the audiobook for English class and followed along in his paperback copy, just like he'd done with Bryan. Sometimes he listened to a chapter twice to make sure he got it. He typed up his homework, which made it easier to keep the letters straight. He cleaned his room, even organizing his maps into labeled shoeboxes on his bookshelves. He didn't plan on taking them out again for a long time. It stung too much to think about his failed adventure and the disappointment of the empty box. He was done with treasure hunting.

Every night, Julian helped his parents set the table and clean up after dinner. Henry was the opposite of helpful. He seemed to make a bigger mess at dinner now that Julian was clearing the dishes. And when their mom and dad asked Julian if he'd finished his homework, Henry chimed in. "Are you sure you didn't miss anything, Jules?"

But Julian tuned his brother out and didn't let it bother him. He was determined not to miss a thing. No more skipped homework assignments, no matter how much they challenged him. Whenever he started to get frustrated, he reached for Star's tag in his pocket to remind him what he was working for.

In the end, Dr. Everett decided to keep Star at the animal hospital for five days. They were the longest —and most exhausting—days of Julian's life. He felt like he had to stay on top of every detail, every minute of every day, or else he'd forget something important. At lunchtime and during their free period, Julian and Bryan spread out their books, trying to get a head start on their homework for the next day. But all they could talk about was the shelter.

Julian hadn't been back to the shelter that week, as he was spending every spare minute with Star. He missed the other animals and the comforting beef jerky treats he gave them and the bright colors of the hallways. Even though Star was safe, he worried about what was going to happen to all the other dogs and cats.

"Ms. Khan said she only has a few more weeks to find the money." Bryan picked the chocolate chips out of his cookie, eating them one at a time. "Pretty soon she's going to have to start calling other shelters to place all the animals."

Julian poked at his cold, leftover pasta with his fork. "Gee—do you know anywhere she might find some money?" He couldn't hide the bitterness in his voice. They both knew there wasn't a buried treasure lying around just waiting to be found.

"I meant she has to raise it," Bryan said. "She has to find people to donate it."

Julian watched his friend take a bite of his now-chipless cookie, and an idea flashed in his mind. "What if we organize a bake sale to help her raise money? I bet lots of people would make stuff to help the animals."

Bryan brightened. "I'm sure my dad would let us set up during lunch. And maybe after school, when parents come to pick up their kids."

"It probably won't raise enough." Doubt crept over Julian. The last time he'd had a big idea, it had ended in disaster.

Bryan seemed to read his mind. "It's a good idea, Jules. Maybe it won't be enough, but we won't know unless we try." He tossed a cookie crumb at Julian. "And no one will get hurt with a bake sale."

Julian thought his friend might not say that if he knew how bad Julian was at following a recipe. But his parents had offered to help him try to save the shelter, and this just might work.

As soon as Julian was done with his homework that night, he brought a stack of his dad's cookbooks to the kitchen table. In his social studies notebook, he started a list of recipes he wanted to make. At the bottom of the page he drew a map of how he and Bryan could arrange the different kinds of treats on the bake sale table. He thought people would buy more if the baked goods were named after animals in the shelter. He came up with Pip Peanut Butter Squares, Buster Brownies, and, of course, Star Snickerdoodles.

Henry came into the kitchen to get a glass of water.

He brought the glass to the table and pulled out the chair next to Julian. As his brother read over his shoulder, Julian braced himself for teasing. He thought his brother would make fun of his handwriting or the names he'd come up with.

"What are you up to?" Henry asked.

Julian lifted his chin. "Bryan and I are organizing a bake sale to help rescue the shelter."

Henry took a slow sip of water. Julian waited for him to say it was a dumb idea or to remind him that the last time he'd tried to bake cookies, he'd forgotten to add the sugar and basically made . . . chocolate chip crackers. They'd tossed the whole batch.

"What happens to the animals if the shelter closes?" Henry said.

Julian doodled pawprints beside his list of recipes. "They don't have anywhere else to go. If another shelter won't take them, they might get put down." He shook his head and tried to shove the thought from his mind.

Henry picked up one of the cookbooks. After a moment he said, "I want to help."

Julian's head snapped up, and he stared at his older brother. "You do?"

"Sure." Henry nodded. "I'll help you bake when mom and dad aren't home. And I bet I can sell a ton of cookies at my school."

"But why?" Julian asked.

Henry flipped through the pages and shrugged. "What you're doing is cool."

Julian was dumbfounded. His brother had never called him cool before.

"Okay, so—here's what I've got so far." Julian showed his brother the list.

As Henry scanned the page, Julian suddenly felt self-conscious. He bit his lip, but Henry set down the list and said, "Looks delicious. I approve."

"Really? Uh—" Julian cleared his throat. "I mean, cool."

"And I can't wait to meet Star," Henry added.

Julian couldn't help but grin just thinking about the dog—*his* dog. It hadn't occurred to him, but that also meant she'd be Henry's dog. Star would be spending a lot of time with his whole family, in fact, so they'd have to get to know her too. "You'll like her," Julian said. "She'll have to get used to you, but she's super smart. She already knows so many hand signals."

"Really?" Henry sounded impressed.

Julian sat up straighter, filled with pride. "I taught her the signals Grandpa used with Liberty. She really pays attention when you know the right way to sign."

"Will you teach me?" Henry asked.

Julian's mouth quirked up in a shy smile. "Will you stop treating me like your stupid baby brother?"

"I'll try." Henry smirked and gave Julian's shoulder a playful shove. Then he got down to business and started paging through the cookbooks. "Are there any turtles at the shelter? We should make mom's turtle cookies."

# ★ CHAPTER 23 ★

**It was a good thing** Star came home on a Saturday, because there was no way Julian would have been able to concentrate in school that day. His parents drove him to the animal hospital. While they talked with Dr. Everett, the receptionist went to get Star. The dog was still moving slowly and limping a little bit, but it was the first time in almost a week that Julian had seen her without the big cone on her head. He knelt on the floor and gently wrapped his arms around her neck. She pressed her forehead against his chest, her tail wagging. Her bandage had been removed to reveal a patch of shaved fur with a line of neat stitches down the middle, as if the map of her markings had been redrawn to show how brave she'd been. She had saved Julian and Bryan.

The receptionist handed him Star's leash and the plastic cone. "She'll have her stitches for at least another week, so she still needs to wear the cone when you're not supervising her. But you can give her a break from it when you're together."

Star rode in the back seat with Julian. It was like they were going in reverse from the night Principal Walter had driven them to the animal hospital, with Star weak and bleeding and her head on Julian's leg. This time, though, she sat on his lap, staring out the window, her bright blue eyes watching the world go by. This was the moment Julian had dreamed about. He was finally taking Star home!

When they got there, Henry was waiting by the front door. He'd arranged Star's new bed and her basket of toys in the living room. "Wow," Henry said, taking a long look at the dog. "She's beautiful, Jules."

Julian was grateful that his brother didn't say a word about the stitches and the shaved patch of fur. Henry got down on the floor the way Julian had shown him and gave Star the special wave that signaled her name. Star cocked her head at the familiar sign coming from a stranger. She glanced up at Julian, a questioning look in her eyes, and when he gave her the thumbs-up, she crept close enough to Henry to sniff his hand.

Star's tail swished in a tentative wag, as if she recognized Henry as part of the family. Julian hoped so. He had a feeling that she would bring them all closer together. In so many ways, she already had.

Ms. Khan had warned Julian that Star might need some time to adjust to another new place. He would do whatever it took to help her understand that this was her home now, that she'd always be safe and loved. He knew they still had a lot of work ahead as she healed and got used to her new life, but he couldn't stop smiling.

For the next few days Julian planted himself next to her dog bed, where he could be close to her while doing his homework and planning the bake sale. And he took her outside every day for short, slow walks. As long as she still had her stitches, they could go only as far as the end of the block. When they reached the corner, she'd lift her snout in the air, her super senses picking up scents and sights all around them. Julian couldn't wait to take her on longer walks to explore the neighborhood.

The day after Star's stitches came out, Julian decided it was time to go a bit farther with her. They wandered the neighborhood, enjoying the fresh air together. Julian was so absorbed in watching Star sniff under hedges and circle around tree trunks, her tail high and alert, that he didn't pay attention to where they were going. They walked a few blocks and turned right, and suddenly they were in front of the Winderhouser house.

Julian had avoided the house since the day he and Bryan planned their treasure hunt on the back porch, but it was just as he'd remembered it. Star remembered the house, too. She gave a high-pitched yip and tugged Julian across the overgrown yard, her ears pinned back against her head. She wove her way around chipped garden gnomes, broken lawn chairs, and plastic milk crates that had tall weeds growing between the slats.

She led Julian around to the back porch and scratched at the back door, nudging it open with her snout.

Julian hesitated. As much time as he'd spent exploring the Winderhouser place, he'd never dared go inside. But he had only a second to decide what to do, as the door began to swing closed between him and Star, her leash pulling taut. She whined from inside, and Julian's mind was instantly made up. He pushed through the door and into the house.

The floor creaked beneath his feet. The house had been abandoned for months, but it was far from empty. Julian looked around as his eyes adjusted to the dim autumn sunlight filtering through the smudged, dusty windows. He could tell from the three ancient refrigerators lined up like sentries along the wall that he was in the kitchen. There were probably other appliances and a sink somewhere in the room, but the counter was piled high with baskets and plastic containers. A bin in the corner had ribbons and rolls of wrapping paper bursting from it like a giant party popper. Towers of newspapers and magazines stretched from the floor almost to the ceiling alongside piles of detached table legs and seat cushions, primary-colored plastic toys, spatulas, a hand mixer, a hair dryer, and other stuff Julian couldn't identify.

His fingers itched with the need to draw what he was seeing. He wished he'd brought along his sketchbook to map out every detail. But Star wouldn't let him linger. She pulled him along a path, threading between piles of boxes and books into the next room. He carefully picked his way around overstuffed garbage bags and teetering stacks of papers, trying not to cause an avalanche. He was so nervous, it was hard to breathe. He didn't want to think about what his parents would do if he got caught trespassing. But he was so fascinated by everything in the house that his mind was spinning. Where had all this stuff come from, and what was it like to live here?

He watched Star step confidently through the house, leading the way. He tried to picture her growing up there and never going outside. She seemed solemn as she sniffed at different objects in the thick quiet of her old home. Julian wished he knew what she was thinking—was she sad? Did she miss Mrs. Winderhouser?

Star's ears perked up and her tail started wagging as she zipped around a stack of newspapers in what Julian thought must be the living room. He followed her into a nook, where a shabby green reclining chair slumped next to a faded blue dog bed that was scattered with toys. Star sniffed the arm of the chair and gave a small whine. Then she pounced on the dog bed. She nosed through the toys, sending a tennis ball rolling under the chair. She snuffled around the bones and toys, her tail wagging furiously. Julian smiled. Star had found her treasure.

She pawed a big stuffed bear out of the way and snapped up a frayed rope toy that had a plush football in the middle. With her favorite toy in her mouth, she trotted out of the nook and back through the house. She led Julian out the back door, down the steps, and all the way around the house to the front porch, where she plopped down next to a rocking chair and chewed happily on the football.

Julian sat down and rocked in the creaking chair.

He gazed out at the street. There were no bears or trains or rivers, but there was still plenty for him and Star to explore. He was content just being with his dog on their daily adventure. He looked down at Star. She was holding the toy between her paws and chewing on the rope, her eyes half closed.

That's when Julian noticed something scratched into the floorboard of the porch, right by Star's paws. He rocked the chair forward and leaned down to get a better look. Star's name was etched into the wood.

He got onto his hands and knees beside the dog. She stopped gnawing her toy and sat up, tilting her head and furrowing her brow at him, seeming to say that he'd better have a good reason for interrupting her. Julian brushed his hand over her name — and felt the board shift under his palm. He reached his fingers into a gap between the floorboards and pulled. The wooden board lifted away, revealing a space below the porch with a metal box in it.

# ★ CHAPTER 24 ★

**Julian lifted the heavy,** dented box out of the hole and set it on the porch between him and Star. He tried to pop the lid open, but it was firmly locked. He didn't want to break the latch this time. Unlike the box in the woods, this one had belonged to Mrs. Winderhouser, and he wanted to treat it with respect. He turned the box over in his hands and found a combination dial on the front.

It was almost as if Julian just knew. Without hesitating, he reached into his pocket for the tag from Star's original collar, which he still carried everywhere. It was the only number the combination could possibly be: Star's birthday. It was his birthday, too. He squeezed the tag in his palm.

"Here goes," he said to Star, spinning the dial clockwise to 11, then the opposite direction to 25, and back the other way to 15.

Julian took a deep breath. The lid popped open.

"Lucky Star!" Julian laughed. He scratched Star behind the ear and then reached into the box.

He pulled out a framed photo of a smiling older woman with short gray hair. She gazed down at a tiny puppy in her arms. The puppy looked at the camera with intelligent blue eyes. Her fur was mostly white, with mottled gray patches on her back, like a map. Even though she was so much smaller in the picture, Julian would know those markings and that expression anywhere.

It was clear from the way Mrs. Winderhouser looked at Star in the photo that she had loved the dog so much. And Star had seemed happy enough in this house, with her bed and her toys. It must have been so hard for her to lose the only person she'd ever known. Then she'd been taken from a home filled with familiar things to a sterile, empty cage at the shelter. No wonder she was frightened and stressed when Julian first met her.

Julian swallowed the lump in his throat and gently set the framed photo aside. He lifted a plain white envelope out of the box and gasped out loud.

Resting under it was a huge stack of cash.

Julian's heart raced, but he made himself open the envelope first. It contained a single sheet of lined yellow paper. Julian unfolded the note and squinted at the looping handwriting.

*To Whom It May Concern:*
*Star has brought me so much joy these past few years. I love her like she's my own child, and I want to make sure she's cared for when I'm gone. I've saved up enough money to take care of Star for the rest of her days. I hope you will love this special dog as much as I do.*
*Sincerely,*
*Rose Winderhouser*

With trembling fingers, Julian refolded the note and put it back into the envelope. He set it aside with the framed photograph and reached into the box one more time. He pulled out a huge brick of hundred-dollar bills.

Julian and Star ran all the way home. Julian clutched the metal box to his chest, worried that it might evaporate into thin air. Star carried her favorite football toy the whole way.

They burst into the kitchen, where Julian's mom had just finished a batch of snickerdoodle cookies for the bake sale. Without thinking, Julian grabbed a cookie and took a big bite out of it, filling his mouth with the warm taste of cinnamon and sugar. This must be what victory tasted like.

"What are you doing?" his mom said with a laugh, moving the plate to the other side of the kitchen, away from Julian. "Those are for your bake sale!"

Julian shook his head and started talking, his mouth still full of cookie. "We don't need a bake sale anymore." He plunked down the metal box on the counter and pulled out the letter, the photo, and, finally, the wad of cash. "Look—this is Star's money."

His mom picked up the photo and looked from the picture to Star. She read the letter, then read it again, shaking her head in disbelief. "Where did you find this?"

"At Star's house," Julian said. "I mean her old house —the Winderhouser place."

"But . . . how?" His mom still hadn't touched the money. She stared at it as though it might not be real. Julian knew how she felt. He'd finally started to accept that there was no such thing as buried treasure, and then Star had led him right to a hidden stash.

"Star found it," Julian said. "We went for a walk, and when we got to the house, she found her bed and all her old toys . . ."

His dad walked into the kitchen and glanced at Star chewing on her football at Julian's feet. "Sorry, did I just hear you say you went into Mrs. Winderhouser's house?" He looked up at Julian, his hands on his hips. "Jules, I can't believe you did that. That's private property, and—"

"Dave." Julian's mom cut off his dad's lecture. His dad looked up and saw the stack of bills on the counter. His mouth fell open.

Julian looked back and forth from one flabbergasted parent to the other. "The note says it's Star's money. So we can use it to take care of her, right?"

"We'll take care of her no matter what," his dad said. "She's part of the family now."

"But—yes, this does seem to be her money," his mom said. "Let's see how much it is."

They sat down at the dining room table, Star lying at their feet with one paw over her football. They carefully counted out the money, then re-counted it because they couldn't believe how much was there: $102,700.

"I can't believe Mrs. Winderhouser had all this cash just sitting in a box under her porch," Julian's dad said with a shake of his head.

But Julian had no trouble believing it at all. He'd known all along that her house was full of buried treasure.

"That'll cover Star's vet bills, right?" he asked.

His dad laughed. "That will more than cover it."

Julian picked up one of the hundred-dollar bills. "So we can use the rest for something else?"

His mom set the letter and the photo down on the stacks of cash and looked at him. "What did you have in mind?"

Julian glanced down at Star. "We want to donate it to the shelter."

Julian's mom stared at him for a second. He bit his lip, worried that she would tell him to put the money back—or that she had other ideas for how it should be used. But the letter made it clear: this was Star's money. And even though Star couldn't talk, Julian was sure this was what she'd want.

"It'll help, right?" Julian asked.

His mom pulled him into a big hug. "It will definitely help. Let's call Ms. Khan right now. You two have saved the day!"

# ★ CHAPTER 25 ★

**Julian had never seen** so many people at the shelter. The parking lot was full, and cars were lining up down the road. The tables set up in the grass were sagging with food, including chocolate-caramel turtle cookies that Julian had baked with Henry's help that morning. Volunteers milled through the crowd, carrying shelter dogs wearing bandanas that said ADOPT ME! A family with two kids chatted with a volunteer who was walking Buster, the kids giggling as Buster licked their hands. Julian crossed his fingers, hoping they'd want to adopt him.

Julian stood with Bryan by the dessert table. His

parents, Henry, and his grandpa sat at one of the picnic tables with Bryan's parents, brother, and sister. Julian and Bryan watched a man with a giant camera interview people as they arrived at the event. The shelter would be on the local news again that night. Over the last few weeks journalists had come to the house to interview Julian and meet Star, and they'd spent time at the shelter with Ms. Khan. The story of Star's buried treasure and how close the shelter had come to shutting down had gotten so much attention that donations started pouring in. Ms. Khan said that Star had helped raise enough money for the shelter to stay open for a long, long time.

"I still can't believe you and Star found that secret hiding place under the porch," Bryan said. "Think how many people walked by there for months, or even years, with no idea it was even there!"

"I wish you'd been there," Julian said. He'd called Bryan right away to tell him the whole story. After everything Bryan had done to help him and Star, it felt like his friend should be part of it, too.

Julian's grandpa stepped between them, balancing a brownie on a napkin. "How's that dog of yours doing, Jules?"

"She's great!" Julian turned to Bryan. "Grandpa is helping me teach Star a new sign to bring stuff to me. I'm hoping to teach her to bring me books so she can help me with my homework."

"I bet we could teach her signs for different books," Bryan said. "Like to get her to bring you the textbook for math or history."

Julian's grandpa nodded. "I bet you could. Just don't blame her for eating your homework."

"I'm hoping to teach her to *do* the homework for me someday." Julian grinned. "Is there a sign for long division, Grandpa?"

"I only got as far as subtraction with Liberty, so if you figure it out, you'll have to teach me." His grandpa winked and went to rejoin the rest of the family at the picnic tables.

Ms. Khan wended her way through the crowd and stood in front of a microphone, next to a large tarp-draped object near the front door. She tapped the microphone a few times, and by the time the third thump came through the speaker, everyone's conversation had died down. The cameraman and local journalists moved to the front of the crowd, pointing their notebooks and phones toward Ms. Khan, ready to record her every word.

"Thank you all for being here today. The shelter and all these amazing—and adoptable!—animals wouldn't still be here if it weren't for your incredible support over the past few weeks. And, as I'm sure you all know, we owe special thanks to one person—and his dog—in particular." Ms. Khan scanned the crowd until she found Julian. His face flamed as he felt the eyes of dozens of people who had turned to look at him. He didn't think he'd ever get used to being the center of attention.

Ms. Khan flashed Julian a wide smile, then tugged away the tarp to reveal a brand-new sign. On it was a beautiful hand-painted rendering of a dog that Julian knew very well: Star.

"Welcome to the Star Shelter!" Ms. Khan cried.

The crowd cheered and whistled.

"Yeah, Star!" Henry shouted.

Julian's parents gave him a thumbs-up—the whole family was using Star's hand signals now.

Bryan high-fived Julian. "That's so cool!"

Julian could only nod in shock. Ms. Khan had cried when he and Star delivered the money. She'd assured him it was more than enough to save the shelter and even make it better than ever. For the past few weeks she'd been cooped up in her office, making plans for what to do with Star's donation. She'd refused to give Julian and Bryan a single hint about what she had in mind.

"We've got a lot more going on than our new name," Ms. Khan continued, holding the microphone in both hands as she looked around at the smiling crowd. "I've been talking with experts across Michigan, and we're developing special programs to help dogs and children in our community. We'll be working with therapists and trainers to create a pet care program to help kids learn responsibility and focus."

Ms. Khan paused while people clapped. "We'll have training classes just for deaf dogs. And we'll develop programs for any dog who needs extra attention. We are going to make sure that every single animal that comes through these doors gets a second chance." The crowd hooted and hollered, and some of the dogs howled along too. "Finally, Principal Walter and I have been working together to start a reading-to-dogs project, where kids can build confidence in reading while helping to socialize our dogs."

This time the crowd went really wild.

"Did you know about this?" Julian shouted to Bryan over the din.

Bryan shook his head. "My dad didn't even mention that he'd been talking to Ms. Khan!"

When the applause died down, Ms. Khan continued. "I'm so excited, because these programs will help our community and our animals. But we're going to need lots of help to pull it off. Please visit the information table to learn how you can be a part of our meaningful work. Thank you all again for your support. I hope you enjoy the food, and don't forget to visit the animals. We have lots of great dogs and cats waiting for their forever homes."

Before she'd even turned off the mic, people began to crowd around the information table. Others were standing in line to take a photo with the new sign. Julian was still trying to take it all in when Ms. Khan approached him. "So what do you think, Jules?"

"It's amazing!" Julian said. "I can't believe all this is happening."

"We couldn't have done it without you and Star. The reporters want a picture of Star with her new sign, but I told them they'd have to wait until after the party. You have quite a celebrity on your hands!" Ms. Khan laughed.

"I'm trying not to let it go to her head," Julian joked. But he was proud of how well Star had been doing with all the attention. She was still shy around new people, but as long as Julian made sure that everyone knew to take it slow and use her hand signals, she didn't get overwhelmed.

Ms. Khan's voice dropped into a more serious tone. "I could really use your help for the next phase."

"My help?" Julian asked. "What do you mean?"

"I'd like you and Star to help out with the deaf

dog training classes. You can show everyone how you taught her hand signals."

"Sure!" Julian couldn't wait to show off how smart Star was and how much fun it was to train deaf dogs. He would've agreed to anything in that moment, though. He was just happy the shelter was still around for him and Bryan and all the animals.

Ms. Khan turned to Bryan. "I'd like your help setting up the reading-to-dogs program. You're already an expert, so you can show other kids how it's done."

"I'll make a plan!" Bryan said quickly. "And a chart with a schedule, so all the dogs who need extra attention get reading time."

"I thought you'd have a plan," Ms. Khan said with a wink. "And I'm hoping both of you will help me out by being a mentor in the pet care program. I think other kids who are struggling in school could really learn from your experience."

"Wow," Julian said, shaking his head in disbelief. He'd never even dreamed that Ms. Khan would forgive him and Bryan for taking Star out of the shelter. And now she was asking for *their* help to help more animals—and kids? It didn't even seem real. "That would be amazing."

Someone called out to Ms. Khan, and she gave a wave at a person behind Julian. "I have to go, but we'll talk more about this soon. Thanks for everything!"

Trying to sort out his thoughts, Julian stared at the grass as Ms. Khan hurried off. He wasn't used to being the one setting a good example. It had been easy for him to focus when he was with Star and doing the things he was good at, but he wasn't sure how he could teach anything to other kids about staying focused in school. He still had to work so hard at it every day.

But he thought about all the work he'd done at the shelter, and how his dedication to Star had helped build his confidence. By being patient with her training, he'd learned to be more patient with himself and with the way his brain worked. He still made mistakes. He'd been so caught up in all the attention on him and Star that he'd forgotten an assignment for school, and he'd needed extra help from his parents to get caught up. And sometimes Star got scared around new people, like when she barked at Henry's friend who came over for dinner. It would never be as easy for Julian or Star as it was for other people and dogs. They needed patience and people who were willing to learn how to communicate with them. It took a while for people to appreciate all the incredible, unique ways their minds worked. But they had each other. They were perfectly imperfect together.

"I'm so excited we're both going to be mentors," Bryan said. "We can come up with a plan for that too. And Star! She'll be like a mentor for the other dogs."

"It'll be fun," Julian said. As long as they were working together, they could do anything.

Bryan ran a hand through his hair. "It might be tough to get other kids as excited about it as we are."

Julian looked his friend in the eye. "We'll be great at it. All three of us."

Julian had never been so proud of himself. Not only had he not messed things up this time, he had actually made them better. And he'd done it by being himself instead of trying to be someone he wasn't. In the end, he hadn't needed a map to find his way. All he'd needed was to trust himself and his two best friends: Star and Bryan.

# ★ CHAPTER 26 ★

**Every day after school,** Julian and Bryan headed straight to Julian's house to walk Star. Then they spread out their books on the dining room table and did their homework. Star brought her favorite football toy into the living room and played with it under the table while the boys studied. Most days they finished their assignments before Julian's parents got home. When their homework was done, they worked on ideas for the new programs they'd be helping Ms. Khan launch in the spring. She had so many new volunteers at the shelter that she'd told the boys to take some time off to work on their plans. Julian and Bryan were also drawing a detailed map of the shelter that Ms. Khan would start giving out to all the new people.

As they walked home, Julian squinted at the flat gray sky. "I wonder if Star ever went outside in the snow," he said. The air was getting colder, and most of the leaves had fallen from the trees. Pretty soon it would start snowing. "I hope she likes playing in it."

"I bet she will, since her fur is so thick," Bryan said. "And we can come up with all kinds of new games for her. We can teach her to catch snowballs and how to ride a sled."

Julian smiled. He was never bored with Bryan and Star around. It was just another average day. Except it wasn't average at all—because Julian had just gotten his very first A on a test.

When Ms. Hollin had set the test on his desk, she hadn't said anything. She'd just winked at him. When Julian flipped over the paper and saw the A, he couldn't help holding it up to show Bryan, who flashed him a thumbs-up from across the room. Only then did Julian realize that everyone in the class had seen his grade, including Hunter.

But before Hunter could say anything snarky, Isabelle leaned forward at her desk. "Nice going, Julian."

"Thanks." Julian stared at the big red A scrawled right beneath his name.

"I heard you're helping out with the new pet care program at the shelter," Isabelle said. "I'm hoping my parents will let me sign up. Maybe you can tell me about it sometime."

"Uh, sure—I'd be happy to," Julian said. He glanced at the back of the room. Hunter sat with his arms crossed, glaring down at his desk.

Julian imagined that his backpack felt different now that it was carrying around an A. It wasn't just the weight of his homework anymore. He had a bubble of success in there, too. He couldn't wait to show it to his family. He knew he owed a lot of it to them.

Julian and Bryan raced up the driveway, as they did every day. They couldn't wait to see Star, and she was just as excited to see them. She was always standing by the door, as if she'd sensed them coming from blocks away. Maybe she somehow knew the minute the final bell rang and they bolted out of school.

Julian dropped his bag and knelt on the floor. Star bowled him over, giving him a million licks and nuzzles. He petted her soft fur and scratched behind her ears and told her what a good girl she was. After she greeted Julian, she ran over to Bryan for more attention, then circled around them until they took her out for her walk.

"Hang on a sec, girl." Julian removed his test from his backpack and set it on the kitchen counter, where his parents would see his A as soon as they got home. He left Bryan with Star while he ran upstairs to get a warmer sweatshirt. When he came back down, Henry was in the kitchen, holding a bag of potato chips and reading Julian's test.

"Great job, Julian!" Henry held up his hand for a high-five. Julian slapped his palm, grabbed the bag from his other hand, shoveled a handful of chips into his mouth, then let Star lick the potato chip grease off his fingers.

"It wasn't so hard this time. I'm really into the book we were being tested on—" Julian didn't think he'd ever said those words before, but they were true.

Reading still wasn't easy, but it was a whole different experience for him now that he'd learned a few new ways to tackle it. "Bryan and I are going to listen to the last chapters after we walk Star."

"Then I won't spoil the ending." Henry handed Star a potato chip. She gobbled it down. "But you'll be really surprised—"

"Stop it!" Julian snatched Star's leash off its hook by the door and snapped it on her collar. He raised his eyebrows at Bryan. "Let's get out of here before he ruins the book."

Henry's laughter followed them out the door. Julian shook his head, but he didn't really mind. Henry had been a lot nicer to him, especially since Star came home. Julian replayed his brother's compliment in his head as he walked down the street with Bryan and Star.

Julian and Bryan had mapped out at least ten different routes around the neighborhood that would take them on different adventures. Today they decided to take the route to the park, where Star could climb on the jungle gym if there weren't a lot of little kids there.

"What did Isabelle say to you?" Bryan asked.

"She wants to join the pet care program," Julian said. "I bet a lot of kids are going to want to do it. Maybe even Hunter."

Bryan shrugged. "Maybe it'll make him nicer. Dogs make everyone better."

Julian agreed. *He'd* sure changed, thanks to Star.

When they got to the park, there was a group of little kids bundled in their fall coats on the playground, so Julian, Bryan, and Star walked all around the neighborhood surrounding the park. The boys talked as Star explored all kinds of smells on their new route.

When they finally headed toward home, Bryan said, "We'll need to map this out. There are probably half a dozen other routes just around this park."

Julian had been thinking the same thing. "It feels like we can keep mapping out our own town for years and still find new places."

"It must have been so hard to be the first people drawing maps, without GPS or anything," Bryan said.

"But so exciting. I'd love to discover something that no one else knew was out there."

"You already did!" Bryan laughed. "I can't believe I'm best friends with someone who found a real buried treasure."

Julian beamed. "Sometimes even I can't believe all that really happened."

They followed Star as she turned the corner and led them onto another new block. She paused to sniff at a fence post, her tail wagging at scents that only she could detect.

"I don't think anyone else in the world could have found it," Bryan said.

Julian knew that Bryan was right. But he wasn't thinking only about Star or the hidden box she'd discovered on Mrs. Winderhouser's porch. *They* had found something special, all three of them. They had found one another.

Julian thought about Star's life so far—growing up in a house where no one knew she lived, being misunderstood at the shelter, facing down a huge bear to save *his* life. Just as people had walked by Mrs. Winderhouser's place with no idea that there was a buried treasure right there for anyone to find, many people had passed by Star without realizing what an amazing dog she was. The same way people had looked right past Bryan and Julian all these years.

Julian felt like he'd struck gold. And now that Star was his dog—and Bryan was his friend—he could barely remember what life had been like before he met them.

"You know, I'm starting to think there's buried treasure all over the place," he said, reaching down and giving Star a pat on the head. "You just need to be willing to search for it." Star looked up at him, her blue eyes sparkling with excitement for their next adventure. As they rounded the corner and Julian saw the Winderhouser place up ahead, he felt in his heart how true that was.

# ★ ALL ABOUT THE AUSTRALIAN SHEPHERD ★

★ The Australian shepherd is a hardworking, intelligent, and athletic dog known for its stamina and trainability. Also called "Aussies," these loyal and affectionate dogs are great companions for high-energy families.

★ The Australian shepherd's origins trace the breed's way around the globe. Back in the 1800s, Basque shepherds living in Spain and France traveled to Australia in search of better fortune, with their best herding dogs in tow. From there, these shepherds settled in California, where admiring cowboys took notice and developed the breed. Though Australian is in the name, the first Australian shepherds were actually born in America!

★ Aussies are incredibly smart and have keen herding and guarding instincts. They're known to herd just about anything in sight: sheep, dogs, even kids! But don't let that fool you into thinking they are single-minded, because they're equally eager to shower their families with love and affection.

★ Australian shepherds have lean, agile bodies and medium to long coats with patterns that often vary, from blue merle to red merle, black, or even red. Most have white or copper patches on their body, which are unique to each animal. They are known for having a penetrating gaze. It is common to see Australian shepherds with light blue eyes, or even a combination of two different colors! Aussies can be anywhere from

18 to 23 inches in height and between 40 and 65 pounds.

★ They love to have jobs, and they thrive in their roles. Many Aussies still herd cattle and sheep out west. Others are excellent therapy dogs, search-and-rescue dogs, Seeing Eye dogs, and more!

★ Australian shepherds have always been popular with ranchers, but they became quite famous for being frequent performers at rodeos! Crowds admire their skill at herding bulls and love the fantastic tricks they can perform.

★ An Aussie is high energy, engaging, and friendly and makes a great pet for a family that has a very active household. A happy Australian shepherd is a loyal, obedient, and animated addition to a family. However, as is sometimes the case with intelligent breeds, they are prone to boredom, hyperactivity, and frustration if they don't receive enough stimulation and exercise. Frequent training and activity are crucial for Aussies.

★ An Australian shepherd that will be living mostly indoors will need consistent bathing and grooming. They have long, fluffy double coats that help keep them warm in the winter and cool in the summer. This also means that they will shed quite a lot when the seasons change. Weekly or daily brushing is encouraged to keep their fur from matting and oil from building on their skin. It will also help keep their fur from collecting on couch cushions!

There is a huge variety of both purebred and mixed-breed dogs available for adoption from your local Pet Rescue. It is really important to think carefully about how your family will care for and interact with a dog so you can choose a breed that's just right for your household. If you have questions about whether a certain type of dog is right for you, contact a local veterinarian or your local rescue, or do a thorough internet search to find the dogs that fit best with your family. This helps keep more dogs from returning to shelters and will help you enjoy a lifetime of happiness with your pet.

# ★ ACKNOWLEDGMENTS ★

The American Dog team is Best in Show! Thank you, Emilia Rhodes, Catherine Onder, Samantha Ruth Brown, Julie Yeater, Celeste Knudsen, Kaitlin Yang, Helen Seachrist, Elizabeth Agyemang, and the wonderful design, sales, marketing, and publicity teams at HMH; and Les Morgenstein, Josh Bank, and Sara Shandler at Alloy Entertainment. Trophies for Agility, Herding, Showmanship, and Best of Breed go to Laura Barbiea, Romy Golan, Robin Straus, Katelyn Hales, Hayley Wagreich, the talented Stephanie Feldstein, Kayleigh Marshall, Rosina Siniscalchi, Ryan Dykhouse, and my dear, wise friend Laurie Maher.

These folks might be tired of hearing how much I love and appreciate them, but too bad. Thank you for everything, Brian, Virginia Wing, Geoff Shotz, Xander Shotz, Katherine Mardesich, Kunsang Bhuti, Tenzin Dekyi, Susan Friedman, and Vida the Great and Terrible.

Turn the page for a preview of

AMERICAN DOG

★ CHESTNUT ★

#1 *New York Times* Bestselling Author **JENNIFER LI SHOTZ**

# ★ CHAPTER 1 ★

"Megan Lucille!" Meg's mom called from downstairs. Her tone told Meg that she had slept in long enough, even if it was her birthday. She could smell coffee and bacon and hot butter bubbling in the skillet. She heard the distant bustle in the kitchen as her sister and brother fought over the pancakes as soon as Dad flipped them onto the platter. Meg knew if she didn't get down there soon, they'd take all the perfectly golden ones. Sighing, she untangled herself from the warm flannel sheets, the heavy quilt, and the fuzzy blanket that wrapped her like a burrito.

She shivered as her feet hit the floor. She quickly found her fluffy robe and pulled on a pair of thick socks. Moving closer to the window, she saw that a crust of snow—maybe an inch or two—had fallen overnight. It sparkled like glitter in the morning light.

Grinning, Meg rushed into the bathroom to brush her teeth and hair. Ever since she was a little girl, she'd been convinced that snow on her birthday was good luck. Now that she was twelve, she was old enough to know it was a silly superstition, but even so . . . it couldn't hurt. Could it? Anticipation bubbled in her chest.

Meg caught sight of her frizzy brown bed head and sleepy face in the mirror. She took a deep breath and reminded herself not to get her hopes up. She pulled her hair into messy bun, then ran downstairs.

"Well, good morning, sleepyhead." Dad laughed as he slid a stack of two pancakes onto Meg's plate. "I thought maybe you were going to sleep all day."

Meg giggled, slathered a thick layer of butter on her pancakes, then drowned them in syrup.

Her older sister, Sarah, looked at Meg's plate and her eyes went wide. "Want some pancakes with that syrup, kiddo?"

Meg just smirked and took a huge bite. It was absolutely delicious. Just the way she liked it. "It's my birthday. You can have as much syrup as you want on your birthday," she mumbled through a mouthful of pancakes.

Sarah laughed. "Birthday or no birthday—we're going to need all hands on deck." She looked out the window. "Sunny days like this always bring the crowds." Sarah was seventeen and the coolest, smartest person Meg knew. She wanted nothing more than to be like her big sister when she grew up.

Their brother, Ben, groaned. "Maybe if we're lucky, it'll start to rain." At fifteen, Ben was slightly less cool and less smart than Sarah, especially since he was always teasing Meg and reminding her that she was the baby.

Sarah elbowed him in the ribs. "Tough luck. It said on the weather app it's going to be sunny all day. Which means . . . Say it with me, Ben."

Ben squeezed his eyes shut and tipped his head back. "Ugh. It means—"

"It's going to be a great day for trees," he and Sarah chanted in unison before bursting out laughing.

Meg watched her siblings and couldn't help feeling a pang of jealousy. She knew that her older brother and sister loved her, but they were closer to each other than they'd ever be to her. It was almost as if they spoke a secret language only the two of them understood, and they could crack each other up with barely a glance. Meg wanted to be part of the club. She wanted them to think she was just as hilarious as they were—and just as helpful, too.

Meg's family owned and operated a Christmas tree farm. They lived in a house on one end of their land and sold the trees from a lot at the front. Meg had been helping around the lot since she was little, but now that she was twelve, her parents were finally going to let her run one of the registers all on her own. Today was her first day, and Meg couldn't wait to get started.

Suddenly, her mom's hands slid over Meg's eyes, and she kissed the top of Meg's head. Meg could feel the rough calluses of her mother's hard work on her hands and smell the sap on her fingers. "Happy birth-day, Meggie."

Her mom uncovered Meg's eyes and there, in the center of the table, was a box wrapped in red and green Christmas paper. It looked big enough to hold a toaster, and it had a bright silver bow stuck to the corner.

For a split second, Meg's stomach tightened with disappointment, then she scolded herself for being so selfish. She couldn't deny the truth, though: there was no way that box held what she really wanted. She'd asked for the same thing every birthday and Christmas for four years, ever since her best friend, Colton, and his rowdy but friendly dogs had moved into the house down the road.

But she'd come to realize that her parents would never get her a dog.

They'd had a family dog when she was a baby. His name was Bruiser. By the time Meg was born, Bruiser was very old. Her family had to scrape and save to afford his medical bills. Her dad was always saying that they would never get another dog because they were too expensive. But Meg suspected that her dad never actually loved Bruiser—not really. And with money being tight, the chances of getting a dog went from slim to none.

"Well, go on, then," Meg's dad said, using tongs to put another slice of bacon on Ben's plate. "Or are you waiting for next year to open it?" He winked at Meg.

She put down her fork, pushed her plate to the side, and tried a smile. She pulled the box toward her and ran a finger across the top of the bow. "Thank you," she said before peeling back the first piece of tape gently.

"Meg!" Ben laughed. "You are the slowest gift unwrapper ever!"

Meg scowled at him, but it quickly turned into a grin. "You know I keep the paper for crafts!" she said, taking her own sweet time. She liked that she did something that made Ben laugh, so she did it on purpose every time she opened a gift.

Her mom sat down on a stool and sipped her coffee. "If you don't like it, we can always return it," she said, watching Meg carefully. "I want to make sure that it's the one you like best."

Gifts were rare in the Briggs family, and even more so for Meg since her birthday and Christmas fell so closely together. She thought she might not even get a present this year. Only after she'd removed the paper without tearing it and folded it gently into a square did Meg lift the lid off the box.

Her breath caught in her throat. Her gaze fell upon a crisply folded, perfect new winter coat. It was bright purple with sparkling silver fur around the hood. Lightly, tentatively, she ran her fingers over the fur.

The last time she'd gone to the mall with Sarah, Meg had touched this same coat. She had imagined, for an instant, how cool she would look wearing it. But she never would have asked for it—it was too expensive, too frivolous. It was the sort of thing she couldn't truly imagine owning, even as it sat on her own kitchen table.

"Oh my gosh!" Meg exhaled, lifting it gingerly out of the box as if it would break. "I love it!" she said, standing up to try it on. "How did you know?"

Sarah laughed. "You made me go back to the same store to look at it four times, kiddo. I figured it was a pretty good guess. Do you like the color? Mom and I had a hard time picking between purple and blue."

"Yes, the purple is perfect!" Meg slid her arms into the sleeves and zipped it up, enjoying the tickle of fur on her cheeks as she pulled up the hood. Then she threw her arms around her mom, whose eyes were glistening as she looked at Meg. "Thank you, Mom. I love it, really."

Next, she hugged her dad. He wiped his hands on the kitchen towel before squeezing her back. "Happy birthday, Megs. I love you, sweetheart."

Meg stood on her tiptoes and kissed his nose. "I love you, too, Dad. Thank you."

She flashed a smile at Sarah and Ben. "Thanks, guys."

"Happy birthday, Meg. Your coat is awesome," Sarah said as she shoved her last slice of bacon into her mouth.

"Yeah, it's pretty cool. Happy birthday, Micro."

Meg frowned slightly but tried to keep her tone light. "Ben, could you . . . would you mind not calling me that anymore? I prefer Meg."

Ben had called her Micro ever since he learned that the word meant very small. Meg used to like it because it made her feel special. But as she got older, she realized that she secretly hated it for exactly the same reason. Nobody else had a silly nickname, but she had tons of them. Her dad called her Megs, and her mom called her Meggie. Colton called her Meg the Leg. But at least those were based on her name. Ben called her Micro just because she was younger and smaller than everybody else.

It was time they took her seriously.

"Sure thing," Ben said with a shrug.

Meg took the coat off carefully and sat down to finish breakfast, her mind purposefully trying to push away a feeling that nagged quietly at her under her excitement. It was guilt. Her parents must have scraped and saved to buy her that coat. She loved the coat beyond words—more than a million thank-yous could ever express. But there was also a pit in her stomach that she couldn't ignore. Her parents needed the money more than she needed the coat. She knew she should tell her mom to return it.

Her mom smiled softly as she held the tags at the end of the coat sleeve. "Well, if you're sure you like it, let's go ahead and cut these off." She pulled open the junk drawer. Meg drew a shuddering breath, knowing it was her last chance to do the right thing.

A sharp snip rang through the air as Meg's mom clipped the plastic tie. Then she threw the tags in the garbage, put the scissors away, and brushed her hands together briskly. "Well, that's that. It's all yours now." Meg smiled, awash with quiet, ashamed relief.

Her dad glanced at the clock on the microwave. "Oh, man. We've got to get to the lot. Gates open in twenty."

Suddenly, everyone burst into action, crisscrossing the kitchen and putting plates in the sink, finishing coffee, filling thermoses.

Her mom glanced at Meg, who was still in her bathrobe. "I'm sorry, sweetie. We have to get going, but we'll have a register waiting for you." She patted her on the arm. She knew how excited Meg was for her first day of real work.

Everyone in the Briggs family loved Christmas,

and Meg was no different. She had always thought that if people could see a Fraser fir decorated with nothing but ice and sunlight, Christmas would change forever. The stores would stop selling ornaments and strings of lights and start trying to recreate the magic of nature.

With sudden awe, Meg realized that her family's farm shared that magic with everyone who picked out a tree there. As a smile spread across her face, Meg felt the possibilities begin to grow around her. The spirit of Christmas lived here. Who knew what could happen?

Don't miss these heartwarming and adventurous tales of rescue dogs in the **AMERICAN DOG** series by **JENNIFER LI SHOTZ.**

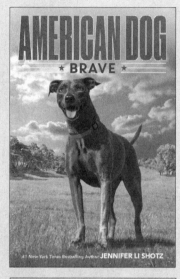

**JENNIFER LI SHOTZ** is the author of *Max: Best Friend. Hero. Marine* and the Hero and Scout series, about brave dogs and their humans. Jen was a cat person until she and her family adopted a sweet, stubborn, adorable rescue pup, who occasionally lets Jen sit on the couch. Jen lives with her family in Brooklyn, loves chocolate chip cookies with very few chips, and still secretly loves cats. Please don't tell the dog. For the occasional tweet, follow her @jenshotz.